Lyric's Accidental Mate

Iron Wolves MC Book 1

by

Elle Boon

Lyric's Accidental Mate

Lyric's Accidental Mate, Iron Wolves MC Book 1
Copyright © 2015 Elle Boon
First E-book Publication: October 2015
Cover design by Valerie Tibbs of Tibbs Design
Edited by Kate Richards of Wizards in Publishing

Dedication

To the best crit partner and truly the greatest lady I've met in this industry...Caitlyn O'Leary. You are without a doubt the best partner in crime. Look out world, we are so going to take over. I honestly don't think I'd be as sane "snort" as I am without your support, friendship, and endless supply of help. I can't thank you enough for all that you've done for me and for all the late night, early morning, phone calls you've taken from this erratic gal. You are my "brain" lol. Tell your hubby thanks for sharing you with me (hehehehe). Truly, I LOVE YOU SOOO HARD <3

There are so many people I'd like to thank, beginning with my awesome beta readers Debbie Ramos, Trenda London, and Jenna Underwood. BIG HUGE thank you to Kate Richards of Wizards in Publishing, you are truly fabulous, and went above and beyond on this book for me. Y'all totally rock and without your input, and help, I'd still be at square one with this book.

Many thanks to my hubby for his unwavering support, my oldest, Jaz for being so damn awesome, and to my Goob who is still my baby even though he's six-foot tall. Without their love and support I'd never be able to do what I love, write.

To the amazingly talented cover artist Valerie Tibbs of Tibbs Design. I love this cover sooo hard, and I know I am now marked down as "that client" with squinty eyes, I Love You.

Chapter One

Lyric Carmichael eyed the trio of giggling women on the dance floor, then looked at her best friend Syn Styles. "Tell me again why we hang out with them three?"

"Should I count them off, or do you just want the number one reason?" Syn sipped on her margarita, laughter sparkling in her blue eyes.

They both knew the main reason they came in a group was their big brothers would never let them come to a nightclub alone, but they also loved the three women. Renee shimmied her ass in a tight red leather skirt against the groin of a random dude, making him grab her around the waist. Lyric watched the couple for a few seconds, making sure her friend hadn't gotten into a situation she couldn't get out of. Only when Renee tossed her long brown hair back, laughing, and the grabby dude eased off, did Lyric turn back to Syn.

"Maybe we should rescue them?" Lyric pointed her beer bottle toward Magee and Jozlyn, who were the center of attention of what looked like a frat party.

Syn looked at her like she'd grown two heads. Renee—better known as Nene—Magee, and Jozlyn were great friends, but they definitely didn't need anyone to rescue them. They'd come to party wearing tiny bits of fabric, while Lyric had on a pair of comfy jeans similar to Syn's that fit like they'd been made for them. Strategic rips kept both just this side of decent. While Syn wore a tight V-necked T-shirt, Lyric wore a tank top with a lace back. Since they'd driven their motorcycles, she and Syn had worn boots, unlike their friends, who were sporting heels that screamed *fuck me*.

"Excuse me, but I like my freedom. Could you imagine the look on Kellen's face if he saw me try to walk out of the house dressed like that?"

She thought of Syn's brother Kellen and the look of horror he'd have, if he saw his baby sister dressed in a miniskirt short enough to show her ass and a crop-top barely covering her voluptuous breasts. Kellen wasn't only the head of the Iron Wolves MC, but he was also their alpha. What he said was law, and nobody, not even Syn, crossed him. Her own brother, Xander—better known as Xan—was his second-in-command, and was just as scary if not scarier. Both stood at over six feet two inches tall, but that's where the similarities ended. Kellen was black haired and blue eyed. He and Syn looked very much alike in their coloring and tall stature, while Xan had blond hair and brown eyes.

"I think we'd have to go into the witness protection plan if we tried it." Lyric laughed.

Raising her glass, Syn clinked her drink with Lyric's. "True that," she agreed.

Lyric got up from the table. "Let's dance, girl."

"Bottoms up, baby." Syn downed the rest of her drink before standing. Their shifter metabolism kept them from getting drunk, but they enjoyed the slight buzz they got from the alcohol, even if it was only short-lived.

They ignored the college guys who called out from several tables as they passed on their way to the dance floor. Lyric was tempted to flip a few of them the bird, or toss a couple backward but restrained herself. "Seriously, do they think yelling hey baby, come sit on my face, will get them laid?" Lyric asked, scooting between the tight tables.

"I'm thinking the answer is yes," Syn tossed over her shoulder.

The DJ played a mix of country, hip-hop, and

3

rock. The song that came on was for a popular line dance that had half the people on the floor sitting down, including Renee, Magee, and Jozlyn. Syn shrugged her shoulders and got in line. Lyric smiled as their three friends flipped their middle fingers from one of the tables, even though she couldn't hear what was said over the music. She got lost in the dance steps, enjoying the beat and movements.

Several songs later, all five of the girls were on the dance floor. Lyric loved letting loose; she loved feeling the loud bass vibrating all the way up, from her toes to her head. She rolled her body with the music, imagining what it would be like if she was with a lover, and thought of the amazing orgasms it would cause. Of course, living with her older brother, she'd not had the chance to experience anything of the sort with anyone, other than her trusty vibrator.

"What's put that frown on your face?" Renee asked.

She bit her lip, but a nervous giggle escaped. "I think it's time for me to get my own place."

Jozlyn and Magee stopped dancing, their eyes looking ready to pop out of their heads. Only Syn seemed to understand her need for independence, since she had just recently been given a cabin by her

4

older brother. It was still on his property, but not in his home. Kellen was giving his sister a little breathing room, unlike Xan, who Lyric swore still thought she was in grade school.

"Xan will never allow that," Jozlyn and Magee said at the same time.

Syn growled at both younger girls. "And when did either of you become so in the know when it came to the second of the MC?"

Oh shit! Lyric recognized the anger blazing in her best friend's blue eyes and was shocked to see it aimed at their friends. If she didn't know any better, she'd think Syn was jealous. Which was absurd, since they each thought of both Kellen and Xan as brothers.

Renee stuck her finger in her ear and shook it. "Excuse me, but did you just growl at us?"

Before a fight could erupt, Lyric stepped between them. "I gotta pee. You need to go with me." She jerked on Syn's arm. By the time they wound their way through the throng of gyrating people and into the bathroom, Syn seemed to get herself under control.

"What the fuck was that all about?" Lyric jerked her thumb toward the closed door and the club beyond.

A deep sigh left Syn in a gush as she leaned against the counter. "I have no clue. There's this wild feeling inside me that seems to be growing lately. I feel like I'm going to snap, and if I'm not careful, I'm liable to bite someone's head off. Ya know?" She placed her palm over her heart, tears swimming in her eyes.

Lyric did the only thing she knew how to do and wrapped her arms around her best friend. "I understand, truly I do. Maybe that's what I'm feeling, too."

"You should move in with me." Syn pulled away, wiping her tears away with the back of her hand.

Laughing, Lyric shook her head. "You think Xan would let me?"

"If it's safe enough for me, then why not you?"

The logic wasn't lost on her; however, she wasn't sure her brother would see it the same way. "When do you move in?"

"Next week. Well, I guess it's more like nine days, but who's counting."

"You owe the Bitches an apology." They were all referred to as the Bitches by their friends; each one had a nickname that ended with Bitch.

"Fuck me running, I know. I was such a beotch."
Syn's voice sounded chagrined.

Lyric walked back toward the last enclosure, she
really did need to go to the bathroom. She shut the
stall door and let the silence stretch.

"You know, you could've disagreed with me," Syn
groused.

"We pinky swore when we were kids we'd never
lie to each other." Lyric laughed when her friend
kicked the door on her way out, calling her a name as
she went.

Straightening her blinged-out belt, Lyric stared
at her reflection. People always assumed she colored
her blonde hair—having dark brown eyes and tan
skin it didn't seem natural—until they met her
brother, Xan. He shared her coloring. Even in wolf
form, they were blonde wolves, a rarity in the wolf
world. Syn and Kellen were both black as night with
the bluest eyes. Alpha eyes. Although, Xan had the
same brown eyes in his human form, when he shifted
to his wolf, his eyes also turned a beautiful shade of
blue, while hers shifted to amber. Had he wanted to
be alpha, Lyric had no doubt he could've been, but
Xan was happy being second. Their parents had been
best friends with Kellen and Syn's, who'd all been

killed ten years earlier.

She shuddered and pushed the memories away, grateful her brother, along with Kellen, had been there to protect her. Xan, all of twenty-five at the time, had been left to raise his fifteen year old sister. Now at twenty-four years old, Lyric felt like the world was passing her by. She'd gotten her degree at the local college instead of going away. Texas was a huge state, but with the club being so tight-knit, and shifters even more so, she'd wanted to stay with her pack. Now she wished she'd at least gone off to one a couple of hours away.

The MC built custom bikes on one side of the shop and was the local mechanics on the other. She and Syn ran the office, while she did more of the creative side of the business.

She planned out what she'd say to her brother about moving in with Syn, and before losing her nerve, pulled her phone out of her back pocket. Knowing him, he'd be with his flavor of the week and not see it till the morning, but at least it would give him a few hours to simmer down before she had to face him, since she was staying overnight at Nene's. Once she hit send, she turned her phone off, and put it back in her pocket.

Butterflies danced in her stomach as she walked out into the dark hallway.

When she got bumped from behind for the third time, she finally turned around and met the steely gaze of a truly mean-looking wolf. She had smelled him and a few of his pack when they came in earlier but hadn't thought anything of it.

"Excuse me, darling. Can I have this dance?"

She saw the way he looked her up and down, stopping at her chest and continuing down to her boots and then back up. "Sorry, I was just going to get a drink." She pasted on a fake smile, trying to step away from him.

His quick-as-a-snake reflexes caught her bare arm, squeezing hard enough to bruise. "Now, that's just rude. I watched you shaking your ass for the last half hour. I think you can dance just one more."

Looking around the crowded dance floor for Syn, Lyric knew she was no match for the wolf, even in his human form. "You are so fucked if you don't let me go. Do you know whose territory you're in?" Although she wasn't strong enough to take him on, any wolf with an ounce of smarts knew better than to come into another's territory and threaten their members.

9

She was technically property of the Iron Wolves; therefore he'd just stepped over the line. If she could get Syn's attention and a little help from her friends, he'd move along, and all would be well. Or she hoped he would.

He leaned in close. "Your little friends ain't gonna help you, bitch."

Lyric tried to pull away from him, coming up against another solid form behind her. "What is wrong with you? Do you know who my brother is? Do you know who the Iron Wolves are? If you let me go now, there will be no harm, no foul. I'll pretend like you don't exist. But, if you keep fucking with me, I will bring the wrath of my pack on all your asses." The last wasn't an empty threat. Her brother Xan would kill any man, or wolf, for putting his hands on her without permission, some even if they had her permission.

"Do you hear her? She's gonna call her big brother." He sneered.

At some point during her struggle with the large man, they had maneuvered her closer to a side hall. If they got her outside, she had two choices. Let her wolf out and fight, or run. Either way, she had little chance of escape. Pack law stated you couldn't show yourself to humans, and the bar was filled with way too many for her to shift inside. She opened her mouth to scream for Syn, or anyone to help her, but one of the men slapped his hand over her lips before she could make a sound.

She counted three men with the leader, but the smells from the bar made it hard to be sure. Lyric pretended to be docile, allowing them to maneuver her outside, while she planned what she'd do as soon as the door opened. She'd only have one chance, and that was a slim one.

The lights from the parking lot speared into her face as someone opened the door before they could drag her outside. "Excuse me, boys, looks like you got a problem there," a man said in a deep rumble.

"Mind your business, punk," the leader growled.

Lyric felt the hair on the nape of her neck stand on end. The man standing by the door was tall and muscular, but was one hundred percent human. She wanted to ask him to help, but changed her mind at the simultaneous growls surrounding her. Although the newcomer was every bit as big as her brother and Kellen, in a fight against a group of wolves, he'd be massacred.

The man held the door open like a gentlemen,

11

nodding as they passed. Lyric had to tilt her head way back to look up at him. The arms holding her captive didn't allow her to do any more than get a quick glimpse of black eyes. She tried to memorize his features, breathing deep to take his scent in before she was shoved outside and the door was shut behind them.

"Beck, I don't think this is the best place for us to take care of business."

She stumbled when the man named Beck released her, shoving the one who'd just spoken against the wall. "Are you questioning my leadership, Raul?"

Claws erupted from Raul's fingers. "Get the fuck off me, Beck. I'm pointing out the fact we should just take the bitch back to the hotel and have some fun with her."

"I agree with jackass, for once. Let's just simmer down. We can take the chew toy and play with her for a while."

Beck released Raul. "Kristof, go get the van and take Raul with you while Dean and I get acquainted with our toy. Call Marcus and have him get word to her brother. I want him to sweat knowing his baby sister is with us, and there's nothing he can do." He turned his cold gaze back to Lyric, licking his lips. "I was just going to kill you and leave you for Xan to find, but plans have changed."

"Over my dead fucking body, asshole," Lyric snarled, unsheathing her claws.

The door to the bar opened and slammed shut. "I don't think the lady wants to go with you."

"Be a smart man and go back inside where it's safe. I won't give you another chance." Beck turned his back on Lyric.

Seeing her opportunity, Lyric nailed Dean in the nuts with her knee and swiped him across the throat with her claws. The wound would be deep enough to immobilize him, but not kill, she hoped. She wasn't sure how long before Raul and the other would be returning with the van, but since the parking lot wasn't huge, she assumed minutes at the most.

Beck turned at the sound of Dean's gasp. "You stupid cunt." The animalistic growl he emitted scared her worse than the thought of what her brother would say if she exposed what they were to humans.

"I've already called 911. I suggest you pick your buddy up and go." The man from the hallway started walking toward them, cell phone in hand, bringing Beck's attention back to him.

13

"Run," Lyric yelled.

The sound of an approaching vehicle had Lyric sprinting away from the downed wolf and the open drive, putting her closer to Beck. An enraged werewolf was unpredictable, but she couldn't allow him to hurt a human. Xan and Kellen had made sure she and Syn had trained with their best fighters, and while she knew she didn't have the strength to take on a group of shifters, she prayed she was able to hold her own against one.

Beck had his back to her, but she could see he, too, had done a partial shift and was facing the gorgeous human. The thought of him harming the man was not something she was willing to allow. Using his distraction, she went low and took out his feet with a swift kick. Man, and wolf, tended to underestimate her because she was small and acted docile. Beck was no exception.

"Aw, fuck," the human rumbled.

At the same time she felt the air stir. Their window of opportunity had passed, and the other wolves had returned.

"Go back inside and find Syn Styles. Have the DJ call for her. Tell her what's happened. Go. Now." Lyric rocked on the balls of her feet, pushing him toward the door with her back to his front.

He snorted. "Sure thing, gorgeous. Just as soon as unicorns fly by."

His big hand came around her, trying to switch their positions. Lyric wanted to snuggle into him. She also wanted to shove him through the door and into safety. As Beck got back to his feet, and the others helped the downed wolf to the van, she thought they were going to leave.

Beck sprang at them with all the speed and strength of a full-grown werewolf on a rampage. She placed herself in front of the human, knowing she could regenerate faster than he could. His hand came around her, trying again to place her behind him. She watched in horror as Beck brought his paw up, claws extended, and hit her with the full force of his strength on the side of her head. Lyric flew across the pavement, head slamming into the concrete wall, making stars appear before her eyes. She wasn't sure what she'd expected, but it wasn't to see her guy ready to take on a shifter. *Whoa, slow your roll.* She didn't even know his name. The hit to her head must have done something to her brain.

Seeing the other two men coming back from their vehicle, Lyric picked herself up. Her main goal was to help the man and hope they got out alive.

Surely, Syn was looking for her by now? The last thought gave her pause. Her best friend would never have allowed her to be gone for so long unless something had happened to her, too. She let more of her wolf out, hearing seams rip and not caring she was ruining a favorite pair of jeans.

* * * *

Rowan swore when the beautiful woman was thrown against the building. Fear for her safety had sent him outside to check on her; seeing her being manhandled by the obnoxious man who needed a shower, sealed the deal.

He'd come to the bar to get a drink or two and get laid. Looked like he was going to get in a fight, and need more than a few bottles of alcohol to erase the images of what he was seeing. Nine, maybe ten-inch nails extended out of the man's fingers, and the last time he'd checked humans didn't have that much hair let alone fur, and the guy didn't have either on his body earlier. In all his training, the wars he'd fought, not a single foe compared to what he was facing.

"What the fuck are you?" Rowan asked, thinking he should've brought his gun from his truck.

Three men advanced on him, looking more like something out of *American Werewolf in London*.

"You should've stayed inside like a good boy," the half-man growled.

Rowan felt the woman step up beside him, easing his fear that she was hurt from being tossed aside. Like all good country boys, he pulled the knife he had strapped to his side. The blade was longer than their claws, which he hoped was enough of an equalizer. She squeezed his free hand, sporting her own set of extra-long nails. Although she was on his side, he hoped.

"Since the lady doesn't want to go with y'all, why don't we skip the pissing contest and forget all about this?" Rowan released her hand, watching the body language of the three man-beasts. They were not experienced fighters, which gave him an advantage.

"There's no reasoning with them. You should've run when I told you to."

He didn't take his eyes off the men as they fanned out in a semi-circle. "Darlin', there wasn't a snowball's chance in hell I was gonna leave you out here to fight off these...whatever they are."

The sound of gravel shifting beneath the man to his right's feet, had Rowan kicking his steel-toed boot into his knee, followed by a roundhouse kick to the head. When he looked down into the face of the man, no longer was there any indication he was human. Gone was the shape of a human face, replaced with the muzzle of what appeared to be one of his worst nightmares. Without hesitation, he grabbed the thing by the hair and cut his throat from ear to ear.

"You will pay for that." One of the beasts' garbled words cut across the night. Before he could hop off the dead creature, he was hit so hard in the side, Rowan was sure a rib or two was cracked.

In his line of work with the military, he'd suffered a lot worse damage and had learned to suppress the pain. His training served him well as he rolled, keeping a firm hold on his serrated knife. Out of the corner of his eye, he watched the woman fighting with amazing skill.

He landed with a thud on his back, momentarily stunned. The large animal on top, snapping at his neck. Rowan grunted in pain from the weight on his ribs, knowing he needed to get the upper hand quickly or he'd be a dead man. What were wolves' weaknesses? Never had he thought he'd need a silver bullet, or wondered if that was a myth or truth. Either way, he was going to die if he didn't get out from under the snapping jaws.

Using all his strength, he heaved, bucking until he finally knocked the wolfman off. Claws slashing his chest as they fought. The burn, like acid eating his skin, made it hard to focus.

Rowan waved his knife hand. "Come on, pussy, is that all you got?"

An enraged howl, and then the animal came at him with more force than cunning.

Rowan sidestepped, slashing upward with his knife, slicing through fabric and tissue. He turned, giving a hard kick to the beast while he was doubled over. Erasing the distance between them, he snapped his neck.

A roar shook the ground. Rowan spun to face the leader, watching in horror as he tossed the woman aside. With a quick assessment, he saw her chest rise and fall.

"I understand it's hard to get laid when you look like you were dropped from the ugly tree, and hit every branch on the way down, but really, there has to be someone out there for you," Rowan taunted him, needing him to come closer, away from the woman. All of the men had partially shifted into part wolf, part man, a seriously grotesque combination.

The beast growled and lumbered on his jacked-up legs. If he made it out of this alive, Rowan was sure he'd be needing therapy for months, maybe years to come.

His side no longer burned, but had started to turn to more of a *kill me now* ache, the likes of which he'd never experienced. He'd been held prisoner for over three months in a foreign land, had been tortured for days on end, and had never wanted to die. Those days and nights were nothing compared to what was going through his system right now, but he fought the pain back. One more to dispatch then he could fall down.

He switched the knife to his left hand, using his right to shield the injured ribs, keeping his eye on his opponent. Basing his decision on the way he hadn't reacted to Rowan's words, except to growl and come closer, Rowan moved forward. A mistake, he realized a moment later, when he was within leaping distance and found himself with a two hundred-plus pound enraged beast on his chest. His knife flew from his hand. All the air left his lungs in a big whoosh, and then the large, gaping mouth that could easily enclose his entire skull, was heading straight for his throat. Rowan reached up with both hands, trying to stop the inevitable, but against the supernatural strength, he knew it was useless.

Not willing to give up and turn his neck for the thing, he stabbed his thumbs into the beast's eyes. Howling, the beast shook him off, but blood ran from the now empty right socket, making Rowan happy he'd at least caused it some damage.

The last thing he saw was razor sharp teeth coming straight for his face. As he grappled with the leader's head, he turned and felt the hot breath on his neck and then pain so immense he yelled out. Black dots swirled in his vision, and then the heavy weight was knocked off him. Rowan tried to get up, but his body wasn't listening to his mind. The sound of fighting brought him out of the daze and or darkness trying to swallow him. He saw the woman holding his knife, her back to him in a fighter's crouch, protecting him. From her posture, he could tell she was ready to kill. His nature wouldn't allow him to lie there and let a woman fight his battles. With the last of his strength, he rolled to his knees. The fight seemed to have gone on for hours, when it could only have been minutes. The sound of a car coming down the gravel drive had all three of them looking in the direction of the noise.

"Your days are numbered, bitch." The leader scooped his two fallen buddies up in a fireman's hold and tossed them into the still running vehicle, speeding away in a spray of gravel.

"We gotta get you outta here." His angel knelt next to him, her cool hand brushing his hair back. Rowan thought he would just lie back and let the darkness envelop him, but she had other plans. "Come on, big guy, I'm going to need you to help me. You're way too heavy for me to carry."

Grunting was his only acknowledgement. What didn't she understand about him wanting to lie down and rest?

"Lava is running through my veins, darlin'. Find my phone and call 911. Find out why they didn't send a car out when I called. That's the only thing that's gonna help me." His voice sounded raspy to his own ears, and lacked conviction. He knew he was dying from the injuries he'd sustained and wondered how she was going to explain to the authorities what had happened.

"Shit, you've been bitten. Fuck, fuck, shit." She leaned forward and sniffed his neck, ripping his flannel and T-shirt down the front.

On the verge of dying, Rowan was amazed to feel his dick harden when the woman licked at his wound, easing the pain. In the next instant, he nearly shot off the ground when her teeth sank into his already wounded shoulder. Instead of more pain, ecstasy rolled through him.

Rowan grabbed the woman around the waist, uncaring about his injuries, making her straddle his thighs. The last time he'd dry humped a female was in junior high with a girl three years his senior. Like then, the girl on top of him panted and climaxed right along with him. Only difference was then, he could get up and get a towel to clean himself. Rowan wasn't sure he could move, let alone get up. Clearly, his dick hadn't gotten the message they were in danger, the way it still pressed against his zipper.

"You two need to get a room for crying out loud." A man's laughing voice jerked him out of his musings.

"Don't move. Wait until he goes inside so he can't see the blood on you."

Rowan didn't want to tell her he didn't think he could move even if he'd tried, so gave a brief nod and stared into her beautiful brown eyes. Her golden-blonde hair fanned them like a curtain, shielding them from others. He wondered what she'd look like spread out naked on his bed and had an answering jerk from his cock. Damn, the thing had never perked up quite so fast before.

Chapter Two

Lyric couldn't believe she'd just had her first orgasm with a man, fully clothed and in public for crying out loud, having just fought off four full-grown shifters. She needed her head examined, but first they needed to get the hell out of there. She didn't bother telling him the police tended to ignore calls unless a fatality was reported. At this point they needed to get him somewhere safe.

When the door to the bar shut behind the couple who'd brought her out of the lust filled haze, she noticed the man beneath her was staring.

"My name's Lyric. What's yours?"

He cleared his throat. "Rowan," he answered. "Listen, I'm not sure what's going on, but we need to file a police report."

She shook her head. How was she going to explain what she'd just done, or what had been done to him. Had she allowed the other shifter's venom to continue flowing through his veins, Rowan would have become connected to him, a part of his pack, whether he wanted to be or not. Lyric had done the only thing she knew would fix it, making him part of her pack. From the moment she'd seen him in the hallway, her wolf had sat up and called to the man, but Lyric had pushed her back. Now, she'd gone against pack law and would have to face not only Kellen, but her brother Xan.

Her wolf beat at her to mark him and claim him as her mate.

"We can't. You know what you saw can't be explained. They'll think you're crazy and lock you up at best. Worst, they'll arrest me and possibly make a lab experiment out of us."

Rowan's grip on her waist tightened almost painfully. "Never. Nobody will ever hurt you."

The fear knotting her stomach lessened, but the urgency to get him as far away from the bar as possible was paramount. She needed a few minutes to figure out where to go that was secure for them both. Somewhere he'd be safe for the change, before she had to face her alpha and her brother. Then she'd offer to let him go free.

She wouldn't mate him. Her wolf whined.

"Come on, help me get you up, big guy." Lyric eyed the gorgeous man beneath her, trying to think how she could maneuver him into a vehicle. The man had to be taller than both her brother and Kellen, putting him at over six foot two. She imagined him on a motorcycle with her wrapped around him. The thought of the tight fit made heat rise to her face.

"If you don't quit looking at me like that you'll be under me in ten seconds flat." His black eyes flashed.

Lyric laughed. "When you're all better, I'll take you up on that offer. Now, let's get out of here." With the agility of her kind, she hopped off him. "Did you drive?"

He got up with a lot less finesse than she'd seem him move with earlier. The wounds from the wolves were already healing, but she had seen humans turn, and he was going to be hurting sooner rather than later. Lyric wanted to find the ones that got away and turn them over to her brother. A shiver raced up her spine. Xan was going to kick her ass.

"Of course I drove, darlin'." Rowan's Texas drawl seemed thicker.

For crying out loud, his voice was panty melting.

"Lead the way, or do you need me to?" Lyric asked.

She snorted at the outraged look he gave her. The overly large four wheel drive pickup truck he led her to, gave her a lady boner. Big trucks, hot cars, and motorcycles were things she enjoyed. Thankfully, the MC had a lot of toys for her to play with. Rowan's truck would definitely fit in. *Back up, girlfriend.* She needed to quit thinking about keeping him like he was hers.

Eyeing the huge leap into his rig, Lyric had visions of her needing some sort of equipment to lift him into the vehicle. He shocked her by expertly maneuvering himself into the passenger seat without groaning or showing the least bit of pain.

Lyric shook her head and went around to the driver's side, happy he had running boards installed, making it easy for her to climb in. Once inside, she held her hand out for the keys. His way too sexy lips tilted up in a grin, before he reached into his tight denim jeans. Her eyes followed his fingers as they dug into his pocket, seeing the bulge still straining against his fly. Licking her lips, she tore her eyes away, only to meet the heat in his. Quick as a snake, his free hand shot out and pulled her to him. Their lips met in a clash of teeth and tongues. There was no finesse, only a deep hunger fed by the fans of heat within her body and his.

Rowan pulled back, blinking to peer at her through heavily glazed eyes. "Darlin', you better start this truck, or I'm thinking we might be christening the backseat."

His words were teasing, but his brow was furrowed and his expression tight. His entire body seemed poised as if he'd toss her over the seat and follow through on the threat at a moment's notice.

A wicked thought of doing exactly what he'd said at a later time—especially since he'd used the words *christened,* meaning he'd never had another woman there—had her smiling slowly. "Another time, big guy."

She took the keys from him before she could change her mind, pulling to the back of the club where her bike was parked. Making a quick decision on how to load her precious baby without the use of a ramp, Lyric circled to the side of the building. After backing up to the ditch that bordered the edge, she quickly climbed out, pulled the tailgate down, and released a sigh. Her calculations were spot on. Hurrying over to her Harley Davidson Sportster, which was far from original, she started the Harley before easing it into the back of Rowan's truck. It took longer than she'd have liked, strapping it with tie-downs.

The poor man in the vehicle had fallen into a

restless sleep, not even stirring when she opened the driver's door. "What am I gonna do with you?" She had an insane urge to run her hand over his beard-roughened jaw. Instead, she put the truck in gear and pulled away from the bar.

Syn had mentioned the cabin on Kellen's land, but that was too close to the alpha for Lyric's peace of mind. He'd smell Rowan on the first stiff wind. She needed time to get him through his change and give him a choice. Stay or go. Mate or no. Even if the last made her wolf whine like a little bitch.

"Where you thinking of taking me?" His voice rasped.

Lyric maneuvered his truck onto the busy highway traffic. "I'm trying to figure that out. I don't have enough cash for a hotel and not sure if that's really a safe place anyways for your first time."

Rowan straightened to look out the window. "Darlin', I'm far from a virgin."

She nearly slammed into a BMW at his words. "Not...that first time. I mean, shit, I can't do this on a six-lane highway." She smacked her hand on the steering wheel.

A pained groan filled the extended cab pickup, followed by a deep exhale. "I know what you mean.

My place is a couple miles down the highway. I think my truck has a mind of its own," he tried to joke.

She glanced over to see his expression in the low dim lights from the dashboard. "You're an ass," she said smiling.

He gave her the directions, but she wasn't properly prepared for the place he called home. Yes, his truck was top of the line and new. However, she didn't expect his home to rival the size of a lodge. "Is this your home?"

"Yes, ma'am."

The man was one shock after another. First with the way he'd handled three full-grown shifters, then the fact he was still alive and talking while being bitten, and now as she stared at the million dollar spread. Kellen and Xan were going to flip their collective lids. "I'm so in deep shit."

Rowan turned his head. "I'll protect you." His tongue peeked out and licked his lips; teeth sharper than normal appeared.

Shivers raced down her spine at the thought of him placing his canines in her throat, or anywhere on her body. She'd heard mated pairs talk about the eroticism of having their mate bite them during sex. She'd love to wear his marks, and wondered if he'd want hers. Her own teeth ached to grow. The bite she'd given him had been to erase the other packs venom—a mating mark was a whole other ball game. One she didn't want to push on him even though her wolf was chomping at her.

"What the hell do you do, Rowan?"

The tree-lined drive was lit up with security lights, but the most breathtaking view came from the wraparound porch. Several wooden rocking chairs with tables between them sat invitingly on one half, while a huge swing hung on the other side.

"Pull up in front. We'll worry about putting this in the garage tomorrow." He sounded exhausted, and she felt guilty for putting him in the position he was in.

"What about my bike?" She never left Pixie out in the elements.

"Shit, I forgot about that. Keep going around to the back."

She did as instructed. The rear of the property was every bit as impressive as the front, with a four-car attached garage. From the middle of the console he pulled a controller and pointed it at the big bay doors. As they opened, she stared slack-jawed at what all he had inside. The boys at the MC would definitely want to come over and play with his toys. If they didn't kill him first.

"Ease in beside the Lexus." His voice came out in a rough whisper.

Thank gawd there was only one open space big enough for his truck. Like she knew what the fuck a Lexus looked like. She was completely out of her league.

With a nod, Lyric coasted Rowan's truck inside. She was so fucked.

* * * *

Rowan had felt Lyric pulling away from him when they'd drove onto his property. He was puzzled by her actions since most women couldn't wait to explore and put their stamp on his home. He wanted to reach over and reassure her, wanted to take her into his arms and tell her everything was going to be fine, but his insides felt like they were on fire. His skin ached from his fingers to his toes. Hell, even his ears hurt. The lights spilling in through the windshield felt like ten thousand watts burning straight into his retinas.

The doors shut down with another press of his

finger to the opener. Before he tried to get out on his own, Lyric was there to help him down. Much to his consternation, he needed the extra help. "Thank you. I swear I'm not usually so needy." Rowan groaned.

Her scent tickled his nose. Sweet strawberries dipped in sin. He loved strawberries covered in whipped cream. Imagining her spread before him, ripe like the sweetest berries, dripping with her own cream, had him pressing her against the side of his truck. "You smell so damn good," he growled.

"Inside, big guy. Let's go." She raised her hands to press against his chest.

He wanted to protest going anywhere that didn't include him in her, until another round of pain hit him. Rowan swallowed the bile trying to rise in his throat and took a step away from the delectable scent of Lyric. The last thing he wanted to do was cause her injury if he lashed out in a moment of weakness. He listened as Lyric gave a brief outline of what to expect. The story sounded like something straight out of Hollywood, but he'd seen the truth for himself. Now, with agony lighting up his insides, he was sure either death was upon him, or she was telling the truth.

"Follow me. I'll show you to a guest suite, and

then you should probably lock yourself in for the night." His words came out less clear than he liked, but he held his head up and focused on putting one foot in front of the other. He placed his hand in front of the scanner, gaining access to his home, and then remembered he had Lyric with him. "Put your palm here." He grabbed her tiny wrist and placed her palm on the screen. A few adjustments, and his system now recognized her palm print as well.

"What the hell was that?" she asked.

"I'm thinking I may be out of it, right?" At her nod, he continued. "Now you can open the doors without alerting the security company of an intruder."

Lyric rubbed her hands together but didn't say another word. Rowan wasn't sure he had it in him to explain further. Hell, he wasn't sure what to expect other than he was going to be turning furry shortly, and if he survived the change, he could still be killed by Lyric's pack.

"You're not going through this alone, Rowan." Her soft hand on his back burned through his flannel.

It took everything in him to continue walking, lights coming on as they entered the kitchen. What did she want him to say? He was raised to protect women and children, not place one directly in harm's way, and the way he was feeling, he was sure she was in danger. "I don't think that's a good idea, darlin'."

"Quit calling me that. My name is Lyric. Not darlin', sweetheart, or any other bullshit name you call some nameless, faceless woman," Lyric growled.

Rowan spun at the challenge in her tone, seeing the glowing amber eyes staring back at him. "Lyric." Her name sounded right rolling off his tongue. "No matter what I call you, the name doesn't matter. All I can seem to focus on is your scent. What did you do? Roll around in a vat of strawberries?"

He watched her expression go from angry, to wary, to alarmed in a matter of seconds.

Her hands rested on the top of the counter. "Shit, this is happening faster than I've ever heard of before."

Lyric put the large granite surface between them, and in his head, he calculated how quickly he could eliminate the space. "I'm going to go shower. You can...make yourself at home," Rowan said.

Lyric nodded but didn't say a word. Rowan could smell her fear and anxiety mixed with the arousal and her own unique scent. He wasn't sure if he'd been hit too hard on the head and all of this was one big hallucination, or if he was dreaming. One thing was for certain, and that was he needed to get away from the woman in his kitchen before he did something he'd probably regret. Like rip their clothes from their bodies and fuck her senseless. Rowan wasn't sure he could actually follow through with the amount of pain he was in, before he fell to his knees in agony.

* * * *

Lyric stared after Rowan as he left the kitchen. Good lawd, he was something. She knew the war he was waging within himself. She just didn't know how to help him if he didn't let her. Being a born shifter, she was strong, but he clearly was going to be an alpha. Already she saw the way his black eyes flashed to blue and couldn't wait to see him shift.

Her ears picked up the sound of running water. She'd never actually helped a human through the change, but from what she'd been told, it usually took a couple days before the full turn. Obviously, they'd never dealt with the likes of Rowan. Damn, she didn't even know his last name.

She pulled her phone out of her back pocket and cursed at the cracked screen and no power coming on. "Shit. What am I going to do? Syn is probably going apeshit right about now." Grabbing the phone off the wall, she quickly dialed her best friend's number. When voicemail picked up on the first ring, Lyric left a brief message outlining what had happened and told Syn she'd call back in the morning. She hoped the other girls were okay and hadn't already called in some reinforcements, and she really wished her phone wasn't fucked up. Another deed to lay at the feet of the rogue wolves. She then dialed her phone number to see if Syn had called and left her a message.

As her voicemail came on, she dialed in the code and listened to several frantic calls from Syn and Nene. Lyric blew out a relieved breath that turned to panic when Syn told her she'd called Kellen. She wasn't scared of her alpha, much. More like freaked he'd put her and the others on lockdown until they found the ones responsible for the attack on her. "Just what the doctor ordered, not. Stuck at the Club with a bunch of overbearing big brothers."

Without pausing to stop, she walked into the living area, lights coming on like they'd done in the kitchen when she stepped into the open space. Modern tech meets country living. The floor-to-ceiling stone fireplace held no family pictures, nothing to show who or where Rowan had come from. When she left the room, the lights went out, leaving the room in darkness. Following the hall leading to where she presumed his bedroom was, she could hear the shower running. The thought of him naked and slick with water made her break out in goosebumps. Never had the image of a wet and naked man brought on such arousing thoughts that she had to force herself away from going to him.

An open door caught her attention before she could act on her impulse to check on Rowan. He had several computer monitors set up on an L-shaped desk. Either the man ran his business from home, or he was a computer geek. Even the image of him wearing a suit and tie didn't lessen her need for him, nor her wolf's. When she moved farther into the room, the lights came on revealing, unlike in the family room, he had pictures lining the walls.

The first one she came to was of a group of soldiers standing next to a military vehicle. Lyric fingered the frame, easily picking out which one of the young men was Rowan. Out of all the smiling faces, his stood out to her like a beacon. Several more framed pictures featured the same group of men, until the last two. Her breath caught in her throat at the images of the men who were no longer smiling, holding a flag for their friend who was no longer with them.

"I see you've made yourself at home." Rowan's voice broke into the quiet room.

Lyric spun on her heel. "For crying out loud, you move quieter than a ghost."

Rowan's smile flashed. "That's what we were. A ghost team." He prowled into the room, sucking the air out of the space with his presence.

She stared at the healing wound on his side, transfixed by the already knitting skin and the amount of bare flesh he was showing in the low-riding jeans. Lyric wasn't sure what the hell was going on, but she didn't think Rowan was normal. Or maybe not completely human. "Rowan, is there something more to you than just...you know, human DNA?"

"To my knowledge, up until about two hours ago, I was all human. Now, I don't know what the fuck I am, except ready to claw my way outta this skin." He held his arms out at his sides.

Not a single tattoo or piercing marked his smooth flesh. She circled him, looking for old injuries from his time in the military. Surely he'd gotten a cut or something that would have left a scar. "Have you ever broken a bone or needed stitches?" she asked.

"I'm pretty tough, I guess. My mama always said I was too ornery to get sick or hurt. She obviously didn't expect me to get bitten by a werewolf. That's what you are, right?" Sweat popped out on his forehead.

He was fighting the pain and stress of shifting. Lyric wanted to call an elder or a council member. Heck, she was willing to call Kellen and ask him for help if it would save Rowan more pain. However, the only thing that would help him now was shifting.

"Rowan, I'm going to need you to trust me. Do you think you can do that?"

He shrugged his massive shoulders. In his shifted form, he would be at least twice her size and could easily dominate her. "Usually this is done with the pack surrounding the new member. The alpha is the one who helps all shifters through their first transition because it's difficult for one to control their beast. I should've taken you to Kellen, but I was stupid and thought we'd have a day or so before I had to admit my mistake to my brother and the alpha. Now, I don't think we have time to do anything except get you through the shift."

He braced his feet apart. "What aren't you telling me, Lyric? Don't mince words or pussy foot around. Tell me what I need to know so I can be prepared."

Taking a deep breath, Lyric laid it out for him. "Once you shift, you will want to hunt. You will want to fuck, and you will most likely want to kill. I don't know in what order you will want these things, but there you have it."

His eyes widened. "What the fuck will I want to hunt and kill? Am I going to go out and take down Bambi, fuck it then kill it and follow up that grand adventure by eating it?"

Lyric laughed. She seriously couldn't believe the things that were coming out of his mouth. "Oh my gawd. You are hilarious." She wiped the tears streaming from her eyes, not realizing he'd began stalking her across the room. Her back hit the wall next to the pictures she'd been admiring.

"Are you laughing at me, darlin'?" Rowan nudged her legs apart, putting one of his between hers.

Looking up into the black eyes of Rowan, she licked her suddenly dry lips. "No, not laughing at you, laughing at what you came up with. I mean, you would probably want to hunt down a deer or two and kill it, but even in your wolf form, you'd never want to have sex with a deer. I don't think even mated pairs have sex in their wolven forms." If they did, she'd not heard them talk about it. She'd never gotten turned on by seeing any of the men in their shifted forms. Beautiful? Yes. Sexy as in she wanted to hump them? No.

"So, you are in danger of me wanting to fuck you after I shift?" He lifted his leg into the V of her thighs.

"Not me, per se. Just that most who are turned tend to get a little out of control." She shivered as he rubbed her in the exact spot that was begging for attention.

"Let me ask you another question." He leaned in and nuzzled close to her ear. "As a shifter, is my sense of smell heightened?"

Lyric tried to keep from rubbing on his steel-hard thigh and to concentrate on what he'd asked. "Everything is heightened. Sight, smell, hearing. Why?"

He braced his arms on the wall, bracketing her head. "Because I can smell your desire. If I was to reach down between your legs, I'd feel you dripping for me. Am I right?"

Knowing her face was bright red and that he could easily see it, she wedged her arms between them, shoving him off her. The movement caught him by surprise, if the look in his eyes was any indication. "Excuse me, but if I was to reach down between your legs, I'm pretty sure I'd feel something hard and it wouldn't be a banana in your pocket. Oh, wait, I don't need to reach down. The little guy is pointing due north. So what?" Fake it till you make it, was her and Syn's motto. "It's called chemistry. Our wolves are calling to each other. It's no big deal. Once I help you through the shift, it'll dissipate." Lyric hoped his sense of smell hadn't become so acute he could tell a lie from the truth like a born shifter.

Rowan turned away from her. "Damn it, I'm being an ass. Forgive me, Lyric. You should go take a shower and then you can help me through the shift or whatever."

She'd hurt him with her dismissal, but his actions scared her. What did she know about him other than he was her mate? Her wolf sat up and yipped at the acknowledgement. Unable to look him in the eye, she walked toward the door.

"For what it's worth, it's a big deal. I've never done this before, Rowan. You called to me when I first saw you in that dark hallway. I'm sorry I got you mixed up in my mess." She fled from the room before he could say anything, hiding the tears streaming down her face. She followed his scent to the last room he'd been in, closing and locking the door to first his bedroom and then the bathroom. The tiled room was like the rest of the house, masculine and top of the line, and showed her just how far out of her league he was.

Lyric fell against the door and slid down until her ass hit the floor. She folded her arms around her knees and let herself cry for a few minutes, then got up and shook out her limbs. "Time to put your big girl panties on and get 'er done." She stripped off her clothes and entered the shower, staring at the high-tech gadgets around the enclosure. "Oh, for crying out loud. Who needs five showerheads?" After figuring out how to turn the water on, she took the quickest shower in history. One day she'd have loved to spend time letting all the different water spouts pummel her body.

Luckily, Rowan had a towel on the heated shower bar. She didn't want to put her dirty clothes back on and figured she'd be having to get naked shortly to show Rowan how to shift, but coming back out with nothing on felt too brazen.

After scanning his bedroom, she pulled one of his T-shirts out of the dresser, and a pair of sweats three sizes too big. He was waiting for her in the kitchen, drinking a glass of water, looking too good for her peace of mind.

Chapter Three

Rowan had to grip the glass in order to not drop it when Lyric returned wearing his clothes. He felt his teeth grow, and the uncomfortable urge to toss her on top of the counter and mark her was nearly overwhelming. The new sensations were taking him out of his comfort zone, and he was never out of control. His world was built on structure and organization. He had a feeling letting Lyric into his life would upset it more than a F5 tornado would.

"Are you thirsty?" His words came out sounding more gravelly than he'd hoped.

Lyric held her dainty hand out and swiped his glass. He watched as she turned the cup and sipped from the spot he'd drunk from, her pink tongue licking where he'd had his lips.

A growl more wolf than man rumbled out. "Girl, you don't want to tempt me too much right now. I don't have a tether on this beast that seems to be growing inside me."

She nodded. "I can feel him reaching out to mine. I've never felt the need to play the way I do right now. Like I want to rub up on you and see how far I can push before you take control." Her head tilted back as she drank the rest of the water.

Rowan tracked her movements, utterly transfixed at the sight of her swallowing, something he'd never found sexy unless the woman in question had his dick in her mouth.

"My skin hurts like a motherfucker, Lyric. Honestly, I can't stand the feeling of anything on me, except I think I could handle having you pressed against me." He smiled when her eyes widened and her scent permeated the air.

"Let's go outside and attempt to get you through your first shift. But, Rowan, I need you to try and remember I'm not the enemy and I'm not up for fucking."

Hearing her say words that belied her body language, Rowan took the glass from her hands. "First of all, darlin', I know you're not the enemy. I'd never want to screw them six ways to Sunday. Second, I'll only fuck you when you are one hundred percent ready and willing. Your body is telling me one thing, your mind another. You are as safe as a nun in a convent." He pressed a quick kiss to her forehead, hearing her breath catch in her throat and her heartbeat increase.

She grabbed his hand. "Come on, big guy."

They stepped outside in companionable silence, his palms sweating while the rest of his body was ready to implode. "Is it like in the movies, where you'll hear all my bones popping and see shit looking all fucked up like?"

"Oh, it's so much worse than that. The first time you'll feel every little snap, crackle, and pop. For those of us who are born shifters, it's not so bad because we shift as kids, and our bones are softer. I've only seen a couple humans change, and let me tell you, I think they wished for death."

"You're not making this any easier." She shrugged and didn't say anything else. The moon wasn't full, so he figured that was another falsehood the movies portrayed. "How about clothes?"

"We most def want to be naked when we shift. Of course, there are times that you aren't able to control your emotions, or so I'm told, and then you end up ruining your favorite outfit."

Rowan looked her up and down. "You mean like you did earlier?"

"That was me protecting you, asswipe. Now, shut it with all the questions, and focus. Your wolf is probably itching to get out." She motioned with her hands.

Rowan felt the other being below the surface but didn't feel threatened by it. "Yeah, it's like he's crouched and waiting for something."

On his back porch, he had a large open area with a fire pit surrounded by low chairs. Off to the side, he had a built-in barbeque grill and pizza oven. He eyed the best spot for his first shift and decided the open yard was the smartest choice. Never one to be self-conscious about his body, he stripped out of his shirt and jeans, leaving his boxer briefs on until Lyric joined him.

A deep exhale and she was next to him, shrugging out of his sweats and tossing his shirt onto the grass, standing in nothing but her perfect, unblemished skin. Rowan couldn't help but stare as she held her head high and her gaze pinned him in place.

"Eyes up here," Lyric said.

He rubbed his hand across his mouth. "You went commando."

Standing there with her hands on her naked hips, Lyric narrowed her gaze. "Your underwear wouldn't have fit me, and there was no way I was putting on dirty ones."

The word *dirty*, coming out of her mouth conjured up all kinds of naughty thoughts, and caused an immediate and noticeable reaction in his briefs. "Eyes up here, darlin'." Rowan teased.

"Kinda difficult when that thing is ready to spring out and bite someone."

"Don't make promises you ain't willing to follow through."

"Stop thinking with your little head and focus. You do not want to end up stuck, shifted in between man and wolf."

Rowan couldn't tell if she was telling the truth or not. Erring on the side of caution, he tore his eyes away from her hard-tipped nipples. He listened as she instructed him on how to find his wolf, and how to let the beast have control, but not to lose himself inside. To say he was scared was putting it mildly.

She agreed to go first, hoping her wolf would be able to communicate with his. Rowan wasn't convinced, but he felt a stirring in his mind. The creature was ready to come out and tried to reassure him. As he watched Lyric shift, he didn't hear her bones popping, but it wasn't a pretty sight to behold, either. It didn't take but a minute before a blonde colored wolf stood where she'd been standing. Before Rowan could reach out to touch her, his own wolf began taking over. He took a deep breath and let go. The pain was worse than he'd expected.

What seemed like hours later but couldn't have been more than a few minutes, he found himself lying in the cool grass, looking down upon paws. There was another being in control of his body, where he was more of a backseat passenger. Rowan remembered what Lyric had told him about asserting his dominance, ensuring the wolf didn't take over completely. An instant recognition flowed inside him.

Once he was sure he could stand without falling over, he got up. He smelled the familiar scent of Lyric close, yet far enough away he was aware she was leery of what his reactions would be. Hunt, kill, and fuck she'd said. He lifted his nose and scented prey near the back forty of his property, close, yet he wanted to run in his new form.

With what he hoped was a nod, Rowan headed off in the direction he wanted to go. They spent a long time running, and then stopped to get a much needed drink at a creek that bordered his land. He nudged Lyric when she got too close to his neighbor's electric fence, scared she'd get injured. Her answering nip to his flank had him turning to nip her back, only to come up short when he scented other wolves. Their howls made the hair on his back stand up, and he sensed Lyric's worry. He wanted to shift and reassure her all would be fine, but those howls were heading straight for them. From Lyric's body language, she knew who was coming, and although they weren't the bad guys, she obviously wasn't prepared for them.

Rowan knew the land like he knew the back of his hand, but, being new to the shifter world he wasn't sure what they could do that he couldn't. Hell, he wasn't positive he could shift back to human yet, let alone on command.

He stood next to Lyric, her smaller wolven body barely reaching his belly, waiting for whoever was coming. They didn't have to wait long before two huge wolves stalked into the clearing by the creek. Rowan assumed the large blond one was Lyric's brother, since he smelled similar to her. The other was a huge black wolf that exuded power and strength. He had no doubt the two men were the most powerful wolves of the pack. He would not show fear to them. The military didn't allow such thoughts, and he wouldn't betray his training tonight.

The black wolf shifted almost seamlessly. "Lyric,

I suggest you shift now, girl. You've got some explaining to do."

Not liking the way the big dark man spoke to his woman, Rowan shifted first, blocking her from their view.

* * * *

Kellen raised his eyebrows at the show of protection. The other man was a little taller than he and Xan, with muscles upon muscles, and not a tattoo in sight. He wondered what the other man was thinking as he stared back at him. Kellen made no apologies for his looks or his behavior. From what they'd learned in the last couple hours, Rowan was a military man with a long list of honors behind him. He'd inherited his home and land and ran some sort of security business. Basically, he was the polar opposite of Kellen and his pack.

"Hello, Rowan. Welcome to my pack. I see you've shifted," Kellen said, indicating the sweat rolling down the other man's temple. Although he was putting up a really good front, shifting hurt like a motherfucker for newly made shifters. Kellen usually connected with his packmates during their first shift and helped them through the pain, taking some of it on himself. As the alpha, he was the only one with the ability to do so, although Arynn, their omega, could also to an extent.

"I don't know the rules. Am I supposed to do something here? Do we see who can piss longer or what?"

"Xan can piss longer, as a matter of fact. Can't you, Xan?" Kellen had felt his best friend shift, but he'd also seen the way Rowan had subtly moved his body, keeping both he and Xan in his sights.

"Let's stop playing games and get this show on the road. Are we gonna kill him or slap him on the back and welcome him with some good ole boy drinking? I'd say fucking, but I don't think I could let him live if he touched my baby sister back there."

Kellen had smelled no mating between Lyric and Rowan, which was good for the new shifter. He didn't think he could keep his second from killing the man if he'd done the dirty with Lyric. Of course, Kellen wouldn't have blamed the man. Lyric was one of the most gorgeous women he'd seen. Sweet, sexy, and sassy wrapped in a small package sure to kick your ass, just like his sister Syn.

"Shift back so we aren't standing with our junk

hanging in the wind," Kellen said. He waited for Xan to shift, knowing his best friend was laughing. "You go first, and I'll help you, and before you say something manly like, *I don't need help*, believe me, you do."

"You really will need his help, Rowan. I can't do what he does as our alpha." Lyric's soft voice broke through their silent stare down.

"Girl, you are so gonna get your ass beat by brother here if you don't quit pressing your naked ass against his naked ass." Kellen warned.

"Technically, it's my naked front against his naked ass," Lyric said but shifted before Xan shifted back to human and followed through with the threat.

Her brother's growl was more anger than menacing, which Kellen understood. If Syn was getting up close and comfy with some nude dude, he'd want to take a bite out of the man's hide, too.

Rowan shook out his hands and rolled his head around like he was getting ready for a fight. He exhaled loudly and then inhaled. Kellen wasn't sure what the fuck the guy thought was going to happen. He'd always been the less talk, more action type guy himself. Without pausing, he opened himself to Rowan, barreling into the mind of the wolf and took over the shift. *Fuck!* Three shifts in one night, and he still had to do it again when they got back to the house. Rowan was probably crying like a bitch and wishing for death right about now. Only Kellen didn't find him cowering in the corner of his mind. The man was trying to handle the pain without showing any outward signs. Obviously, Uncle Sam's training was paying off.

After he made sure Rowan could hold the shift, he opened a connection to all three of his pack members. *All right, my minions, follow me and don't fuck around. I'm not in the mood to hunt, kill, or fuck Bambi. Dude, that is messed up on a level even Bodhi ain't messed up on.*

Xan nudged him in the side. *Who wants to fuck Bambi? Unless she's some new hot chick?*

What is going on? Why can I hear you in my head? Rowan asked.

That's the power of the alpha. Sorry, I sorta screwed you by not taking you to him for your first shift. I just thought we'd have a few days. Lyric's voice sounded apologetic.

We will talk about it when we get to Rowan's. Kellen didn't allow any room for arguments. With Xan taking the lead, he nipped Lyric, letting her know

57

without words he wanted her to follow. Rowan, still in protective mode, would follow, of that Kellen had no doubt.

He understood more about Rowan in the moments he was inside his mind than he'd ever get talking to the man for days or weeks in a deep interrogation session. The man was definitely in lust with Lyric, and, if he wasn't missing his mark, they were meant to be mates. Things were about to get interesting. He kept his chuckle to himself, knowing his best friend was gonna be one pissed off big brother when he realized his baby sister was about to be mated.

At the back deck, Xan shifted quickly, holding out a blanket for Lyric as if he wanted to hide her nudity from Rowan. Kellen wanted to laugh at the audacity of his second. They were naked more often than not, especially when they shifted. The fact he was acting like the big brother who was protecting his sister's virtue was comical. Kellen wondered if Lyric would do the same if roles were reversed. He pictured what she'd have done if she'd seen Xan fucking the chick before they'd gotten the call about the attack at the bar. He already knew what Lyric would've done, and the answer was the same as Syn. Nothing. They'd walked in on more than one woman bouncing on their brothers' dicks and done nothing more than tell them to wear protection, or lock the door next time.

Lyric ignored Xan's outstretched arms and pulled on what was obviously men's sweats and shirt. Xan growled, but she folded her arms and glowered at him. Kellen ignored them and focused on helping Rowan do his final shift of the night. The man may be the most stoic male he'd ever met, but he was still newly made. Using his connection he took on some of the pain and helped Rowan focus on becoming human once again.

They shifted at the same time. Kellen was there to catch him when Rowan stumbled, his strength finally giving out.

"Fuck, I feel like I was waterboarded and left for dead." Rowan scrubbed a hand down his face.

"That happen to you often? The waterboarding thing?" Xan asked.

"Shit, I...forget I said that."

Lyric handed Rowan his jeans, as a mate should do, in Kellen's mind.

"All right, let's take this party inside." Kellen swiped up his own pants, putting them on and checking his cell phone. "Shit, we got trouble." He showed Xan his phone. They had a text from Arynn that one of their females was missing. "Change of plans, kids. Lyric, I know you've got Pixie here somewhere?" At her nod, he looked at Rowan and knew the man was in no condition to drive. "You want to leave her here and drive him, or you want Xan to drive your guy back to the clubhouse?"

"I can drive myself. Or, better yet, I'll just stay here," Rowan said.

Kellen looked down where Rowan had parked his ass on the first step. "Sure thing, and flying monkeys are coming out of my ass. What's it gonna be, Lyric?"

"How did you find us?" she asked.

"We have a locator on all the vehicles. Before you ask something that will more than likely piss me off, no, we don't check up on you girls. It's for emergencies only." Kellen took in her mutant expression.

"I never unloaded my bike from his truck, so I'll drive us." Lyric dug her toe into the ground.

He nodded. "You will follow me, and make no detours, little girl." Kellen didn't think she'd disagree with him or challenge his authority, but, just in case, he made sure she understood it was an order.

"Do we have time to pack him a bag, Alpha?"

Snark rang clear in her voice.

She didn't wait for him—he didn't expect her to. Rowan watched her stomp into the house, and Xan couldn't hide his amusement either.

"Someone needs to put her over their knee," Kellen growled.

Rowan pulled himself up off the step. "Nobody will be touching her."

Kellen laughed as Rowan got up in his face; his threat held real heat. Yeah, he was going to make a great addition to the pack, once he found his place. "Boy, you ain't big enough to take me on today. Now, settle down and wait for Lyric to come back with a bag so we can scat."

"Shit, he's got some balls. Maybe we need to see how he does in the ring against one of us." Xan rubbed his hands together.

Kellen grunted.

* * * *

Lyric heard her brother talk about getting in the ring with Rowan and thought they'd all be in for a big surprise if they did. Xan was a dirty fighter, but her guy was tough as any she'd seen. He'd definitely give them all a run for their money.

She wondered if Syn was aware they LoJacked their asses? In Rowan's room, she found a duffel in his closet, quickly grabbing a couple pairs of soft jeans and T-shirts, throwing in a few pairs of socks and boxer briefs. The man may go commando, and look great naked, but she didn't want him to think she was a perv. A smile curved her lips.

"What's got that smile on your face, darlin'?"

"Shit, I told you not to sneak up on me." She dropped his bag. "Here, since you're clearly well enough to carry your own stuff. I haven't gotten any of your bathroom supplies."

Rowan bent and picked up the duffel. "I'll just grab a few things. I think I'm ready to wake up now."

"What?" Lyric asked.

He shook his head. "This whole thing seems surreal, and although I find you to be the embodiment of sexy itself. I really think I'm over this dream." He turned and walked into his bathroom.

Lyric watched him enter, her heart breaking at his words. He'd only wanted to help a woman out, and instead, his entire life was turned upside down. Now, he was wishing he'd never met her. He may not have had a choice in becoming an accidental shifter, but he didn't have to be her mate. She would let him go, even though it would kill her to watch him pick another. Now that Kellen had accepted him and was willing to teach him everything, Lyric would let Rowan choose his own path. Nobody wanted an accidental mate thrust upon them. She wanted a man who chose her, not one who didn't have any other choice.

With her decision made, she wiped her fingers under her eyes and strolled out of his bedroom for the last time. By the time she got to his big truck, she had her breathing under control and her mask of indifference on.

There was no way he was going to be able to drive. She'd seen his hand shake when he'd picked up the bag. Climbing into the driver's seat, she waited for him to make his way out. Her breath caught as he emerged in a fresh pair of jeans and another button-down. He'd also put on a pair of boots. Gah, she loved cowboy boots on men. As he engaged the alarm system by the garage opening, his back was to her, and she watched the flex of his ass in the denim. She was going to lose her sanity if she had to watch him hook up with one of her friends. Or she'd end up killing the woman, or women who made a play for him.

"I see you're doing the driving?" He raised his right brow.

Lyric pressed the button on the door opener. "Obviously. Buckle up, buddy." No more using cute little pet names. She was putting him in the friend zone.

Sitting idle in the circle drive were Kellen and Xan with their custom bikes rumbling. They were enough to keep her mind on the task at hand. Kellen's skullcap and facemask covering was scary as fuck, partnered with Xan's, and most people on the road gave them a wide berth. She laughed at Rowan's shocked expression.

"Aren't they worried they'll get pulled over when someone calls in about bikers wearing skull and crossbones on their faces?" Rowan asked.

"Nope, they've been pulled over many times. The masks keep the dirt and dust out of their eyes, nose, and mouth. Police can't argue with logic." She followed the bikes.

His grunt had her thinking of other times he would make that sound. To stop her mind from going there, she turned the radio on, tuning to her favorite station that played rock. He relaxed in the seat, the stress from what he'd gone through finally catching up with him. Kellen's bike pulled first onto the highway, while Xan hung back. They were making sure nobody was following them. Something she'd not thought to check on since seeing them. This late in the evening, there weren't a lot of vehicles on the highway, but still enough it made it hard to discern if anyone was tailing them. She was glad her brother had her back. Rowan, for all his strength, was in no shape to take on anyone at the moment, and she couldn't truly fight off more than a wolf or two and hope to survive.

Lyric had fucked up by taking Rowan home instead of to the Iron Wolf. Kellen wouldn't have punished her or Rowan for what was done. Her wolf wanted him, and she'd been too stupid and selfish to think straight. Now, he was paying for her selfishness. Had she taken him to see Kellen, he'd have been welcomed into their society with open arms. He'd have been helped through his first shift by the alpha, cutting down on the pain and agony and wouldn't have had to go through so many shifts in one day. Instead, she'd fucked him over royally, and he didn't get to do the top three things all shifters wanted. Hunt, kill, and fuck.

"What's wrong, Lyric?" Rowan asked.

His words jarred her out of her thoughts. "What? I thought you were sleeping. Are you okay?"

Rowan's hand settled on her thigh, making her tremble. "I could feel your...I'm not sure what it was, but it made me and my other aware. Does that make sense?"

Lyric jerked her eyes from the road to look at Rowan's glowing blue gaze. "Don't look at me like that, Rowan."

"Like what?" He licked his lips.

She put her hand over his where it lay on her thigh. "I didn't mean to wake you. We're almost to the clubhouse," she said, not answering his question.

He turned his hand over, entwining their fingers. "Tell me what to expect once we get there. Are they going to put me through my paces and make me fight for my place? You know, like only the strong survive or some shit?

His thumb rubbing along her palm almost made her forget what he was asking her. "What? God, no. Rowan, you are pack now. I know you didn't want this, and rest assured we don't go out and just turn people. As a matter of fact, it isn't done. Usually there is a process and a petition before a human is ever turned. I've never heard of this happening with someone without their consent and knowledge. The only time someone becomes one of us is if they are mates. Had that other wolf not bitten you, I'd never have...done it. I couldn't allow him to make you his. You saw how Kellen could go into your mind?" She waited for him to squeeze her hand. "The other wolf, if he was the alpha, could've done the same at any time. If he wasn't the alpha, then whoever was his alpha could've done the same. They can control you to an extent. You are strong, so I don't think you personally would've been susceptible, but imagine some weak human."

"Holy shite. I never thought of that. Do you think he can still get into my head?" Rowan released her hand. The loss of his warmth made her ache.

"No. Kellen would have felt another presence inside you when he took over your shift." She wished he'd reach back out and touch her, but he stared out the passenger window, lost in his own thoughts, or so it appeared.

"I want to find that fuck, and kill him," he growled.

Lyric nodded, but they were pulling into the lot of the MC. Dozens of bikes and cars were still there.

Lights flooded the parking lot with music blaring, letting her know there were still many of the members partying. Exactly what she needed.

Syn stood with Nene near the entrance, their worried expression easing as they saw her driving the truck and her bike in the back. Rowan sat up straighter.

"Stay by my side, Lyric. Don't leave me, okay."

Her heart melted at the plea in his voice. "I'll do my best, but remember Kellen is the alpha. I have to listen to him and so do you."

She pulled his truck into an open spot and turned the key off, gasping when he pulled her over the console in the middle to sit on his lap. "I don't give a flying fuck what he is. You are mine. You stay with me. We clear?"

The electric-blue eyes worried her. Alpha eyes. She couldn't let him go into the Iron Wolf showing signs of an alpha like he was ready to challenge Kellen. "Rowan, listen to me. I want you like none other." She shifted, straddling his lap. "Inside the club, Kellen is top man. We all listen to him. He won't make me or you do anything that puts us in danger, nor will he do anything he truly doesn't think is best for all of us. Right now, you only think you want me.

Remember what you said back at your house? Give it time. We will see what you really want. Just don't do anything that pisses Kellen, or Xan, off. Okay?"

The heat from his body under her was stirring things inside her she wished they could act on. Her canines ached to sink into him again, only this time marking him for the world to see.

"You mean like rip your clothes off and fuck you senseless?" Rowan asked.

Damn, her pussy actually pulsed at the imagery of his words.

A growl brought both their heads around to the driver's side. "That would definitely get you in some serious trouble," Xan said.

Lyric stared at her brother, could see he was deadly serious. "Oh, for the love of all that's holy, Xander. I've caught you too many times to count, so stop acting all...whatever you are."

"You're my baby sister. The last thing I want to see, hear, or think about is you getting fucked. Now, let's get inside and I'll have one of the guys unload your bike."

She looked around for Kellen, figuring he might be around to talk some sense into Xan, but their fearless leader was nowhere to be seen. Choosing the safer route, she pulled the door open on the passenger side and climbed out ahead of Rowan, smirking over her shoulder at Xan.

Bodhi was at the door, looking as menacing as always. With his bleached-blond hair shaved at the sides and spiked on top, and his dark skin and tattoos, he looked exactly what he was. A total badass ready to kick ass now and take names later. He was also a total sweetheart when it came to the ladies. He flashed his pearly white smile and twin dimples. Since coming back from the desert with his smokejumper friend Slater, he'd been a little more protective of all the women in the club. Lyric couldn't wait to meet the men she'd heard about who had the ability to read minds, create fire, and other cool shit. She figured they might need them in the future.

"Good evening, sweets. I hear you've been out causing trouble as always." He pointed one thick finger at her. The rings he wore on his right hand, had, on more than one occasion, caused a lot of damage to men too stupid to watch their mouths. "Kellen and your friends are in his office. He said to bring our new member along." He looked Rowan up and down. "You need some ink."

"Thanks, Bodhi. Did Syn and Nene seem okay?"

She put her body in front of Rowan. Bodhi had always enjoyed watching her and the other girls dance. She hoped he would focus on her instead of Rowan. The tilt of his head let her know he saw right through her actions.

"Syn, of course, was worried. Nene, too."

The way he said Syn's name had her taking a second look at his expression. He'd never let on that he was interested in any of them, other than he appreciated beauty. Bodhi was a ladies' man, which was why they all steered clear of him. He never had just one woman on his arm, or in bed, it was always two or three. Lyric and her friends did not share. Ever. If he had his sights set on Syn, she'd have to warn her best friend to watch herself.

Chapter Four

Rowan could feel the stares of everyone as he and Lyric entered the bar. The Iron Wolf MC was more than just a motorcycle club. They clearly had their own bar, and from what he'd seen, they did custom bike and car work in another building. He'd have to do some investigating, if he lived long enough. The one named Bodhi was a big son of a bitch. His assessing once over didn't seem to miss anything. He'd not smelled any interest in Lyric coming off the man. How he'd been able to decipher that particular scent, Rowan wasn't sure, but it settled his wolf enough he was able to look the other man in his shades-covered eyes.

In the darkened atmosphere with the flashing lights and the heavy pumping music, Rowan wondered why Bodhi had the shades on in the first place. The black T-shirt with the clubs logo stretched tight across the man's muscles. He assumed he was the bouncer, and since he had to top Rowan, and his muscles seemed to have muscles, he was probably pretty effective. The huge stainless steel rings on his hands probably hurt as much as the punch, if the man decided to throw down. Rowan filed all the info away for future reference. At the mention of Rowan getting a tattoo, he balked. In the military, they never put anything on their bodies that the enemy could use to identify them. He was no longer in covert missions, but the training was there nonetheless.

"Come on. Let's go see what Kellen has to say."

Seeing Lyric hold her hand out to him, he took it and pulled her into his side. Bodhi may not have looked at her with lust in his eyes, but he saw several others staring at her like they'd like to eat her up. He liked that she was wearing his clothes, carrying his scent.

She melted into him, making both man and beast relax.

"Lead the way, darlin'." He released her hand to hug her, his arm going around her waist to rest possessively on her hip.

He'd felt her pull away from him at his home, and he didn't like it one little bit. He wouldn't allow her to put space between them, figuratively or physically. If he had to chain her to his side, he would.

She sidestepped the crowded dance floor, which

was as different from the other bar as night was from day. Here, the scantily clad bodies did more than just bump and grind. He was sure there might have been some actual fucking going on if he was to look closer. Possibly some threesomes. Rowan heard more than a few moans and some *fuck yeah, babies*. A few other words and expletives had him making a quick decision, Lyric wasn't allowed to come here alone ever again. Not without him. She took them down a long hall and stopped outside a huge door with a wolf carved into the wooden surface. Knocking three times, she entered without being told it was okay.

Inside, Kellen sat on a black leather sofa, his arms stretched across the back, looking relaxed, one booted foot crossed over his knee. His eyes, however, held a different message. "Have a seat, both of you." He indicated the couch across from him.

Rowan took in the room filled with a total of four black leather sofas and a leather coffee table in the middle. He wondered how many couples had been back here and then decided he really didn't want to know. Off to the side, a big desk with a state-of-the-art computer sat, indicating the MC Pres was up-to-date on technology at least. His jeans had been swapped out for a pair of black leather pants that laced up the front, and a matching vest with a wolf's head on the upper right corner. The club's logo was above it with the word President in block letters below, letting everyone know exactly who and what he was.

As soon as they entered, her friends jumped up and pulled Lyric from him. Rowan wanted to protest, but with the intent look on Kellen's face, he relented. She gave him a quick introduction, which he filed away.

"Now what?" Rowan looked Kellen in the eye.

"Did you recognize the men who attacked you?" Kellen asked.

Rowan shook his head. "No. Never seen them before. I'd gone to the bar for a drink and had just gotten there when I spotted Lyric being strong-armed out by four men."

Kellen rested his elbows on his spread knees. "How did you know it wasn't a lovers' spat?"

He heard the other women gasp, but ignored them. "There was desperation in her body language. I'm trained to recognize these things. I decided I'd let them think I was no threat and continued on into the bar and let them take her outside. I figured I could easily take on four men. Of course, I had no clue they'd be turning into wolves ready to tear my guts out." He copied Kellen's relaxed posture, resting his arms across the back of the sofa.

"Kellen, it wasn't Rowan they were after. I was the one they were specifically targeting in the bar." Lyric spoke up, telling them about the incident on the dance floor. She sat next to Rowan, close enough her thigh pressed to his.

The one named Syn raised her hand. "I got distracted because someone had drugged Magee. Luckily our systems don't react the way humans do, but she was violently ill. I assumed you were on the dance floor still. I'm soo sorry, Lyric. Had I thought you were in danger, I'd never have left you that long."

"Where is Magee now?" Lyric tried to get up, but Rowan held her to him with one arm around her shoulders. Kellen's eyebrows rose at the display.

"She's at home resting," Kellen answered.

The door opened and in walked Xan. He kicked the door shut, unfazed by the glower on Kellen's face. "Please respect the door, brother." Kellen waved his hand imperiously at him.

"Screw off," Xan said heading over to the opposite side where a small semi-circular bar sat. The chrome design fit in with the black furniture.

The door opened again, and a gorgeous blonde
with purple and pink curls walked in singing the
lyrics to "Sex Metal Barbie" by In The Moment,
looking every bit the part.

"Really, Breezy. Don't you know how to knock?
And, for the love of all, who let you out of the house
in that?"

Rowan was sure he could hear Xan's back molars
grinding together. He glanced at the new woman
named Breezy, and had he not had eyes for only
Lyric, he was sure he'd have been drooling over this
one. Her white corset pushed her ample breasts up
while showing off her tiny waist. The miniscule
denim jean skirt looked like it had been cut off, but it
covered her ass. It was probably the knee-high
stockings that did it for Xan, with the lace tops
playing peek-a-boo when she walked. Her hips
swayed as she sang the words about being a harlot
and a homicidal queen.

She batted her obscenely long lashes at Xan.
"Why, my daddy even gave me a pat on the head and
told me to be a good girl tonight. I told him I was
always a *good* girl."

"Enough you two. I don't need your version of
foreplay tonight." Kellen pinched the bridge of his

nose. "Breezy, is there a reason you came to see me?"

"Yes, Alpha." She walked over to where Kellen sat, pulling something out of the top of her corset.

Rowan heard Xan moving before he saw the other man actually clear the space. One minute he was a good ten feet across the room from Breezy, the next, he was beside her, taking her hand in his.

"What the fuck are you doing?" Xan asked.

Rowan couldn't see her expression, but he felt Lyric tense.

Breezy elbowed Xan in the stomach. "This note was left on my windshield. I was waiting until you got back here, Alpha, to bring it to you. You must've slipped in while I was...busy."

"Busy doing what?" Xan gripped her by the arm.

"Listen, Xander Mother-Fucking Carmichael. You don't own me. You have no right, so back the fuck off me." Breezy twisted in Xan's grip.

"Not on your life, bella." His hand tightened.

Rowan was ready to come to her defense, but Kellen spoke up first. "Xan, leash your wolf. Breezy, let me see what you got. Did you notice anyone around your car?"

The blonde shrugged away from Xan. "I didn't, Alpha. I'm sorry. I ran into the store to get some gum and came out to find that note."

"Sit down. You're both making my neck hurt."
Kellen sat forward and read the note. "What the fuck
does this even mean? *Your blood will become my
blood*?"

"Why didn't they try to take her, like they did
Lyric?" Rowan asked then watched as Breezy spun
and nearly toppled over before planting herself next
to Kellen, much to Xan's displeasure.

"Oh, crap. I never thought of that. Do you think
they followed me here? Or are waiting for me to
leave? I mean, the store parking lot was full of people,
so maybe that was why they didn't try anything."
Breezy's voice shook.

Kellen patted her knee. "It didn't matter at the
bar where they tried to take Lyric, but maybe a
parking lot full of humans who weren't intoxicated
stopped them. Do you remember anything out of the
ordinary?"

"I remember the feeling of being watched, and
looking around before I spotted the note. I thought
some guy was trying to hit on me."

"Does that sort of thing happen to you a lot?"
Xan sat on the sofa arm next to where she sat.

Breezy adjusted her top. "More often than I like,

yes."

"Do you think it has anything to do with the way you're dressed?" Xan questioned, curling a strand of pink hair around his finger. Rowan watched the tightening of the blonde's shoulders.

"I had a jacket on over the corset, zipped up, for your info. Besides, I should be able to go out wearing this and not have to fend off some asshat. You should be whipped for suggesting I brought on any bullshit by the way I dress." She jerked her hair free.

"Bella, I like to do the whipping, and I promise you'd enjoy the fuck out of it," Xan said.

"Back to the problem at hand. Whoever left the note was probably watching you, Breezy. More than likely, they watched you come here, but that's okay. It's not like we hide our club. Bodhi would've recognized a strange shifter walking in." Kellen drew their attention back to him with his growled words.

Rowan agreed. The man at the front door looked as if he'd not miss a damn thing, but Rowan wanted to check over the entire premises. He wouldn't trust Lyric's safety until he was able to ensure it himself. *Shit.* He was already becoming possessive of the woman. He hoped she didn't mind because he didn't see it changing any time soon. He'd even let the man named Bodhi ink him if it meant he could lay claim to Lyric.

"Can I go home now? I'm feeling kinda ill." Breezy got up off the couch.

"Have someone follow you, and let your dad know what's going on. He and your mom need to be on guard. I know you work at the hospital, but be alert when you come and go. Don't go anywhere alone. You hear me? If I have to, I'll put Xan on as your guard."

She nodded. "Coti said he'd take me home."

"Fuck that. I'll take you home." Xan stood.

"Xan, I need you here since Taya's missing. I need you and Bodhi, along with Arynn. He can sense her, and so can I. That means she's still alive." Kellen pinned Breezy with his blue eyes. "Coti is to take you straight home, no fucking off."

"He's my friend, nothing more." Hurt laced her words as she pushed up from the couch.

"Then he shouldn't have any problems getting back here quickly," Xan said.

Breezy walked around the ottoman, ignoring Xan. "I'm glad you're okay, Lyric. Welcome to the pack." Her friendly smile was genuine as she looked at Rowan.

"Thank you, Breezy. I'm sorry my brother is an ass." Lyric squeezed her hand.

"It's okay, I have become immune to his lack of charm." Tears sparkled in her eyes before she blinked them away.

Rowan could smell the lie and hear the hurt in her voice. At the door, Breezy looked over her shoulder. "By the way, it's not Coti you should worry about me fucking, Xan." With those words she walked out the door, her head held high. Rowan hoped like hell he never pissed Lyric off to the extent that Xan clearly had Breezy.

"Who the hell is she talking about?" Xan asked Lyric and Syn.

Syn lifted her shoulders in a negligent shrug. "We don't necessarily run in the same circles, you know. Breezy and her girls are a few years older, and are a little more...adventurous than we are."

"What the fuck does that mean?" Xan snarled.

"I don't give a flying fuck," Kellen roared. "Stop thinking with your goddamn dick, and either let the woman bounce on your cock, or deal with the fact she's one hot piece of ass any man, or woman would be glad to have."

Rowan felt Kellen's power flood the room. No

wonder nobody questioned the man's right to rule. Rowan felt like turning his head and giving him his neck. He barely restrained himself, but noticed Syn and Lyric weren't so brave. Xan met his gaze across the room. He lifted one blond brow.

"Looks like we have another alpha, Kellen." Xan stared at Rowan.

Kellen smirked. "If you'd had your head outta your ass, you'd have noticed that earlier."

Xan lifted his middle finger and then went back to the bar to pour himself another drink. He held up the bottle, and Kellen nodded.

"You want one? It's the good stuff, Maker's Mark," Xan said.

"Throw it over some ice for me." Lyric leaned forward with a smile.

Syn got up and poured another drink while she got Lyric's. Rowan nodded and then accepted the glass.

He went over the events again from when he'd spotted Lyric and the men at the bar, to the fight and what the van looked like. At the last moment, he remembered the downed man hadn't been killed, only two of the four.

"Was there any signs of the altercation at the bar

when you left?" Xan asked.

"Only the faint scent of blood. Whoever these guys are, they called for a cleanup crew. Meaning they had this planned." Kellen looked over at Lyric.

"They didn't plan to take me, though. They called me a chew toy and specifically said they wanted to get word to you, Xan. Like this is a personal vendetta."

"Fuck!" Xan slammed his fist on the counter.

"What aren't you telling me, Xan?" Kellen asked.

Xan downed his glass of amber liquid. "Taya and I've been seeing each other. Not exclusively, but I did stay at her place night before last."

"Who the hell did you piss off? It seems this is aimed at you. First they take Taya, then they attack Lyric and leave a note for Breezy. How the hell do they know who you're connected to?" like he was ready to spit nails.

"I've no damn clue. Taya and I are casual. Lyric is my sister, and I'd kill for her. Breezy is...well she's just a chick in the club. I'd protect her like I'd protect any pack member."

Rowan wanted to snort.

"Is there any other *casual* relationships that these fucks might target?" Kellen got up and started pacing.

The glass cracked in Xan's hand. "Don't act like you don't have a different woman every night, Kellen. I'm single, healthy, and can't help it if there is a line of ladies willing to, as you so eloquently put it, bounce on my cock. You're exactly the same, so don't even think to condemn me, brother. Just tell me what I need to do. You want a list of every woman I've fucked or had suck me off? Give me a pen and paper."

Lyric got up off the couch. "I think this is our cue to go."

"I want you both to stay here at the clubhouse in one of the suites. Don't worry, there are some that are freshly cleaned." Kellen smirked.

Rowan got up to stand next to Lyric. "How safe are we here?"

"Safer than you are away from here." Kellen answered.

A deep growl echoed around the room. "They're not staying in the same suite." Xan moved around the bar.

Kellen got in front of him. "You and I have some work to do and a lady to find before someone else gets hurt. Taya may not be your *mate*, but she's someone's. Let your sister help Rowan get settled while you use your nose and head."

Xan inhaled, making Rowan think he was ready to explode, only his eyes flared and then rested on Lyric who flushed a rosy red.

"Motherfuckingsonofabitch," Xan said.

"Exactly." Kellen slapped Xan on the back.

"Well, all right then. We will go find that clean suite. Err, thanks for the hospitality," Rowan said.

There were some undercurrents going on, but for the life of him, he had no clue how to decipher them. Lyric grabbed his hand and led him from the room, but not before her friend Syn kissed her cheek and hugged her. Rowan didn't understand these wolves and their touchy-feely selves.

He was onboard for touching and feeling Lyric. The idea sprang into his head as they left the office and wouldn't leave. They didn't go back through the crowded bar. Lyric kept hold of his hand that didn't have the duffel bag. He felt a little panicked at not having a hand free in case they came up against any threat. She clearly knew where they were going, taking a few turns through the darkened hallway, steadily going down until they hit a steel door with a keypad. He watched her enter the code, memorizing the number.

Rowan adjusted her stance. "You need to make

sure you put your body in front of you when you enter the code. That way anyone around or behind you can't see what the access number is. I now have the key to get in should I want to come back."

"Jeezus, what are you, some sort of security expert?"

"Yes, ma'am."

"Seriously?" she asked, pushing open the heavy door.

Rowan approved of the security they had in place; they only needed to teach everyone how to enter the code without broadcasting what it was.

To the right of the dimly lit hallway was a reception area manned by an elderly couple.

"Hiya, Mrs. McCartney. How are you feeling this evening?" Lyric smiled.

"Lyric, you know how it is. Today is good. You wanting a suite for your friend?" Mrs. McCartney asked.

Rowan suppressed his chuckle. "Evening, ma'am. My name is Rowan. Kellen wants us to stay here for a day or two. I hope you don't mind." He tipped an imaginary hat at the elderly woman. He was sure she saw all kinds of comings and goings through these halls.

"Well, now, missy, why didn't you say the alpha sent you both down here. I have the perfect suite for you. Not one of the ones the boys usually use, either." Mrs. McCartney sniffed.

"Now, honey. You know them boys are just playing until they find them someone like you. They gotta look under a lot of pots until they find their gold." Mr. McCartney winked at Rowan.

"Hmm. How many pots did you look under, dear?" Mrs. McCartney opened a safe and pulled out a key.

"Not many. You were waiting right there, my love. I've been living in bliss ever since." The old man winked again. Rowan turned his head and coughed into his hand.

"You okay there, young man?" The older man asked with a twinkle in his eyes.

"What? Oh, yeah. Just had a little something in my throat."

The woman gave them a key and explained there was water in the fridge. Lyric thanked her and pulled him along the tastefully done hallway. He couldn't imagine Xan or Kellen bringing strange women past the elderly couple.

"You're wondering how Xan and Kellen could

bring some piece of ass past those two, right?

"Yep," he said as he followed her into their rooms. He looked around the space they were to share for however long Kellen decided. A large living space with a couch and two chairs opened up to a kitchenette with a counter doubling as table, with two barstools in the main room. There was a door off to the side he assumed led to the bedroom, and when Lyric opened it to deposit his bag, he saw the huge king-sized bed.

"Are you hungry? There's a full service kitchen that will make us anything from burgers, to steak, to mac and cheese and such. Don't expect gourmet shit, but they can whip up some really tasty barbeque."

"What are the sleeping arrangements, Lyric?" Heat raced through him just thinking of sharing a bed with her.

"Um, since you're bigger than me, you can have the bed, and I'll take the couch." She nodded.

"What if I wanted the couch?"

Her puzzled frown made him want to laugh. "Why would you want the—"

Rowan closed the space between them, and took her lips in a kiss that he'd been dying for since the last time he'd tasted her. She tasted like the whiskey

90

they'd drunk. He traced her lips with his tongue, dipping inside and rubbing alongside hers.

He pulled back. "I don't want the fucking couch. I want you, Lyric. God, do I want you." The admission was ripped from him.

She licked her lips. "I want you, too. So much it hurts. Are you sure? I mean, it could just be your wolf."

"Back at my place, I felt him clawing at me, but he's quiet now. It's me who wants you. Is it you or your wolf who want me?" If she said her wolf, he wasn't sure if he could pull back.

"Me. I mean, my wolf wanted you, too, but she's not saying a word right now." Her face flushed.

"Good. Hold that thought." Rowan wasn't sure how she'd react to what he did next. Years of training didn't allow him to relax until he'd checked out the area. He did a perimeter check. Only one way in and one way out. He placed one of the barstools under the door handle as an added security measure. Lyric stood rooted to the spot he'd left her in.

"All secure, soldier?" She stood at attention.

Rowan placed a hand on either side of her ribs and lifted. "Only as secure as you want it to be, darlin'."

When Lyric wrapped her legs around his waist and locked her ankles at his back, he swore nothing was sexier.

"I like living dangerously." She tugged his T-shirt off and tossed it to the side.

Her beautiful, bra-less breasts were too much for him not to take into his mouth. Her intake of breath pushed her closer to his face, and he took that as a good sign. He released her nipple with a loud pop.

With her wrapped around him, he took them into the bedroom. The bed had been done in a red, white, and black color pallet. The black wood furnishings looked heavy and expensive, with a white bedspread, several red throw pillows, and other splashes of red throughout.

"I hope you like the room?" Lyric asked.

He realized he stood holding her for far too long, making her apprehensive. "Darlin', the room could be a dirt-floored shack, and I wouldn't notice as long as you were there."

She blushed. "Do you realize you make me wet with your words alone?"

"Let me get you out of these sweats and see for myself."

Rowan laid her on the bed, but when she went to

remove the pants, he stopped her. "Let me. It's like Christmas. I get to open up my present."

Lyric tossed her hand above her head. "If you take too long, I might just start without you."

"You know what happens to bad girls?" Rowan tugged off one of Lyric's shoes and then the other, before he tucked his hands into her elastic waistband and pulled, knowing she had nothing on under them.

She shook her head at his question.

"They don't get to come. In fact, they get spanked. Have you ever been spanked, Lyric?"

He could smell her arousal increase at his words.

"No. I mean, my dad did once, but—" Lyric let out a gasp.

Rowan blew on her exposed pussy. He loved that she hadn't waxed or shaved herself completely bare on top. Spreading her lips apart he found her clit was already exposed and red, and he knew she'd come apart with only a few swipes of his tongue. Her inner thighs were soaked. He ran his fingers through her sweet cream, tracing the outer edges before testing her readiness.

She bucked against him. He tapped her mound, making her still. Going back to tracing circles around her clit, he carefully avoided touching the bundle of nerves.

"Do you want to fuck my fingers, Lyric?"

She squirmed at his words. He wondered if any of her previous lovers had ever talked dirty to her. Using his index finger, he scraped his nail across the top of her clit.

"Fuck me, Rowan. With anything. God, I just want to come."

He settled down between her thighs, spreading them farther apart. He lapped at the juice running out of her pussy like a starving man. "Not yet, darlin'. I don't think you're ready yet."

"The fuck." Lyric reached between her legs.

Rowan stopped her palm from coming between him and his treat. "What did I say?" He held her hand in one of his, while he gave her mound a firmer tap. "Now, keep your hands above your head, or I'll tie them up." More of her sweet arousal permeated the air. She may have never played before, but she enjoyed what he was saying and doing to her. Rowan rewarded her by licking a long swipe from her pussy to her clit.

"Yes, oh, Rowan. Right there." She panted.

"If you do as I instructed and be a good girl I'll make you come so hard you'll forget your own name."

Her entire body shuddered, but her hands stayed in place.

Rowan nipped her inner thigh then licked at the mark, tasting her there. He could become addicted to all the flavors of this woman. He worked his way up her legs, licking and sucking every bit of flesh he came into contact with. Her pussy lips were so smooth, he wondered if she'd had waxed or had some sort of hair removal, Rowan wasn't sure which, but was grateful. He made sure to pay proper homage to each one, taking it into his mouth and licking with care that had her thrashing on the bed.

By the time he inserted one finger into her pussy, the inner walls were already clenching. She was so tight around the one digit, he wasn't sure how he'd get his dick into her. A few orgasms, he hoped, would make it easier because only an act of God could keep him from fucking Lyric.

He pumped in and out and sucked her clit into his mouth at the same time.

"Fuck, yes, I'm coming," Lyric screamed.

Easing a second digit in, Rowan scissored them back and forth, stretching her little by little while she rode out her orgasm. He kept his fingers inside, but released the bundle of nerves, knowing it would be ultra-sensitive. He looked up Lyric's body and would have sworn his heart stopped beating in that moment. Her arms were thrown above her head, a beautiful smile graced her lips, and her eyes were closed. A woman who trusted her partner would catch her if and when she fell. Rowan wanted to be that man for all time. His wolf woke up and gave him a silent nudge. His gums ached like he should allow his teeth to grow. An overwhelming urge to crawl up Lyric's body and slide his cock deep inside her pussy and bury his teeth in her neck nearly had him pulling his fingers out and doing just that.

"Again, Lyric. I need to feel you come again." She was so tight, he feared hurting her with his size.

"Inside me this time, Rowan."

Rowan pumped his fingers, adding a third. "I need to make sure you're ready."

She gripped his hair. "I passed ready a few minutes ago."

Chapter Five

Lyric looked down at the man who appeared prepared to spend the rest of the night between her thighs. Lying on top of the white comforter, she thought of all the debauchery they were going to do and hoped Mrs. McCartney forgave her. His large fingers felt great inside her, stretching deliciously, but she wanted his big cock. She wondered if she should tell him she'd never been with a man before.

"What about protection?" Rowan asked, swiping his tongue across her again.

Fuck, how can the man think of practical things? "There are things you'll learn. One, we aren't susceptible to human diseases. Two, we are only fertile twice a year. You and every other wolf will know when a female is in heat. It's very similar to other canines, only we don't need a dozen wolves to service us. We are just able to get pregnant at that time. Now, can we proceed?"

Heat lit his gorgeous eyes. "We will revisit this conversation later."

She liked his possessive attitude. The way his

words rumbled against her was another sensation in itself. "Okay, so will you fuck me now?"

"You are so going to get your ass spanked." He growled.

"Promises, promises." She squeezed her inner muscles around his fingers, hoping it would get him to move up her body. His eyes flashed from black to blue, and she feared she'd pushed him too far.

"Up," he ordered, removing his fingers and body from hers. She felt herself being lifted and the coverlet being tossed to the foot of the bed. "Lie in the middle, and don't touch yourself."

Wow. Rowan was a totally demanding lover. She had never had a man, or wolf, tell her what to do like he was, but found she loved it. She'd never had a lover, so maybe they all did this. Somehow she doubted they all were like Rowan.

Watching him strip off his shirt, she was amazed at the flex and play of muscles. He tossed the flannel to the side then lifted his arms and pulled the undershirt over his head from behind. She loved how guys did that, the way they crossed their arms and effortlessly did the task was sexy as all get out. His jeans came next, and, with a tug, he pulled the sides apart. Gasping as his cock sprang free, Lyric licked her lips, imagining wrapping them around the mushroom-shaped head.

"Don't do that or I'll come all over your tits and then you'll have to go get clean and I'll have to start all over."

"That doesn't sound like a threat to me."

He groaned. "You're going to fucking kill me. Maybe your brother should've locked you away."

Lyric grabbed her breasts and tweaked her nipples. "What fun would that have been?"

Rowan's grip on his dick looked painful, but he placed one knee on the bed and then the other. "Darlin', I'm beginning to think I didn't know the meaning of fun before you."

His words sent warmth through her.

He settled on top of her, and she shifted her legs farther apart, raising them to rest against the back of his thighs.

Rowan held himself up on his elbows, looking down on her with a strange expression.

"What are you looking for?" she asked.

With a shake of his head, he brought his mouth down to hers. Lyric had been kissed before. Many times, but none had ever felt like a claiming the way Rowan's kiss did. He turned his head and changed

99

the angle of the kiss, sucking her lower lip into his mouth, and then did the same to the top. Good, lawd, the man was making love to her mouth.

He shifted, and she felt his cockhead brush against her pussy. She thought he was going to push into her, had hoped he would, but the diabolical man had other plans of torture. He continued to kiss her as if he had all the time in the world, rubbing her pussy with his dick, waking up her nerve endings all over again. She shifted, trying to force him to enter her.

Rowan chuckled against her mouth. "So impatient, luv."

She didn't take his word to heart. It was too soon, but she was sure she was on the cusp of falling hard for this man. Her wolf, and her own silly self, wanted to claim him for their own, but she made a promise. She would give him a chance to...decide what he wanted. Even if that was another woman, Lyric wouldn't kill the faceless bitch. She'd try really hard not to hurt her too badly.

"Hey, where did you go?" Rowan asked.

She smiled and tried to shake off the fear he'd choose another. "Nowhere. I was just worrying about everything."

"I must not be doing this right then." He sighed.

Lyric wanted to tell him it was her not him, but then he began nibbling on her neck. She loved having her neck bitten just right. Nobody had ever done it the way he was, with just enough pressure she actually felt her body responding with little tremors. "Oh, fuck me."

Rowan chuckled like he knew, which he probably did with his heightened sense of smell.

He didn't break the skin, but Lyric felt his teeth and was aware she'd have a visible mark and loved it. When he moved down to her upper breast and bit down again, she shivered. If he continued, she'd explode into a million little pieces. His stubbly chin scraped across her nipple, eliciting a moan and another streak of heat went straight to her core. Lyric was on the verge of begging him to bite her, mark her, and fuck her as he sucked the tip of her left breast into his mouth. She howled and was sure everyone in the compound heard her. Her back bowed off the bed; her nails raked down his back. He did the same to the right one, scraping across her nipple.

Lyric couldn't handle any more. She rolled them, using her strength and his distraction to her advantage. "Can't take anymore. Need you inside me, now."

"Take what you need, darlin'. I'm all yours," Rowan said, holding Lyric by the hips as she gripped his dick.

She guided the tip to her, taking him inside. God, he was so big. She pressed down, taking a little more, then lifted back up. Her hands on his chest, she rocked back and forth with his hands on her hips, helping to guide her.

"Too slow, Rowan. Help, me. I want all of you." She was panting.

Sweat beaded on his brow. "Is this your first time, Lyric?"

Her teeth tugged on her lower lip. "Technically, yes. I mean I have BOB, but he doesn't really count."

Rowan nodded and flipped them, his cock sliding out of her. "It's okay. Trust me."

With her on her back and him looming over her, she saw how tightly he was holding himself in check. He braced one arm next to her head, the other he used to guide himself into her. Slowly he worked his way inside, his thumb flicking her clit with each pass, taking her close to the edge again. The man was a fucking god in bed. She flinched at the sting of pain which was quickly erased as Rowan worked his magic.

Once he'd worked his entire length in, Lyric stared into his dark eyes. "You feel so good inside me." Her battery operated boyfriend was getting the boot when she got home. The pain was subsiding as her body adjusted to his size, making the need for more apparent.

His cock twitched. "My dick agrees. I don't want to move." He rested his forehead against hers. "I'd ask how you stayed a virgin so long, but I'm chauvinistic enough to be one happy motherfucker right now. Plus, I've met your brother."

Panting, Lyric nipped his chin. "Let's not speak of the devil." She swiveled her hips. "Hmm, I kinda like having you right here, but I really need you to move."

Rowan laughed. "Your wish is my command."

Lyric thought she was ready for him to move, but nothing could've prepared her for the sensations he awoke as his dick moved in and out of her. His arms came down and wrapped around her shoulders, bringing them chest to chest. Her nipples lit up at the contact, making her pussy squeeze in counterpoint.

"Fuck, don't do that. I won't last," Rowan

growled.

Pulling his hips back, he set up a fast and furious pace she met with her own. She couldn't hold back the orgasm that washed over her, any more than she could her teeth from coming out. Rowan's eyes widened, and his own teeth appeared. She tried to tell him it was normal, that she had been told it happened during sex, but he growled a deep animalistic sound.

"Mine," he said and then bit into her shoulder. Another orgasm, harder and even more intense, rolled through her.

"Yes." Lyric agreed. Her own wolf yipped and struck into his exposed shoulder.

Rowan howled, his hips slamming into her, and he shouted as he came. They each licked the other's wounds, their bodies shuddering in unison.

Lyric wasn't sure what to say to him. How to explain they'd just marked each other and were forever mated. He didn't understand the way of their kind. There were no divorces like humans. She'd just royally fucked up, and he was already growing hard again. Her body responded, wanting him again.

He rolled. "Ride me, this time. I want to see these bounce." He tweaked her nipples.

She knew it was the coward's way out, but they couldn't undo it and he had bitten her first. Tomorrow she'd tell him what it meant and hope he forgave her. Everything always looked better with the sun shining.

"With pleasure." She smiled wickedly, moving back and forth in a slow glide. Every movement made her more aware of the way he filled her so completely.

By the time they fell asleep in an exhausted heap, Lyric had it worked out in her mind what she would say to her mate when they woke up. She wouldn't beat around the bush, she promised.

Lyric woke with a start, knowing instinctively something was wrong. She looked around the dark room for Rowan. The silence that greeted her had unease skating down her spine. She didn't call out for him like a damsel in distress, knowing he was not in the suite.

Opening her senses, she half shifted to allow her wolf out in order to sort through the layers of smells and noises. The older couple were sleeping soundly, if the noises coming from the large apartment were any indication.

She dressed in her discarded clothes from the

night before when there was no sign of her mate. He'd fucked her into the wee hours of the morning, yet he had the audacity to leave without a word? Her wolf wanted to rip his nuts off, but her human heart felt like it had been ripped out.

The door he'd wedged a barstool under was locked, but not secured like he'd left it the night before. Another pang hit her heart that he didn't take measures to secure her like a mate would. She tried to tell herself he didn't know all the rules of shifters, but the excuse was lame even to her own mind.

Rowan's faint scent didn't head back the way they'd come; his trail led toward the outer doors that were so heavily coded she was sure he'd be there since he didn't have the access to get out. The lights flickered in the dimly lit hallway, an eerie sense that something was not right warned her to sound the alarm, and then the smell of Rowan's blood hit her.

Her mate was in trouble. She tried reaching him through their bond, coming up blank. The thought that he was too injured to answer had her stumbling against the wall, then common sense made her reassess the situation. Rowan was still newly made and hadn't fully bonded with his wolf. Taking a deep breath, she centered herself.

Kellen had strict rules when it came to pack. Her mate, new or not, was one of theirs. She took a moment to call out to Kellen, their link as strong as if he was right in front of her.

After ensuring the pack was made aware there was trouble at the MC, she looked out through the camera screen mounted on the wall, searching the empty parking lot for any sign of a disturbance. Seeing nothing, nor any indication of where Rowan had gone, she threw the door open, coming to a stop at the small drops of blood. Her mate had been injured outside the sanctuary. She kept her back to the door and squatted, seeing the clear imprints of several boot prints. The fact they were boots, and not paws, led her to believe it was men, not wolves.

Her alpha's presence floated over her long before he actually stepped out the door.

"What the hell is going on, Lyric? Where's your mate?" Kellen's blue eyes flashed as he scanned the darkness. She'd never truly been scared of her brother's best friend and the alpha of the Iron Wolves. Being eleven years older than her twenty-four years, he was like another big brother. Kellen was the alpha everyone feared. His six foot two frame had already began a partial shift, making him even larger. Black claws that could rip a person's head from their body extended from the tips of his long fingers. His deep voice sent a chill that had nothing to do with the night air down to her toes.

Voice quavering, she answered. "I woke to find Rowan gone. When I followed his scent, it led me here." She pointed to the blood and scuff marks.

The tunnel leading back up through the back entrance shouldn't have been found by anyone, not even another shifter, unless someone from their pack had betrayed them.

"It doesn't look like he shifted, but I can smell wolf other than your mate. I want you to go back inside and set the alarms. Do you understand me? That means everyone inside is to go on lockdown." He touched her arm, the contact gentle, yet commanding.

Lyric wanted to protest that it was her duty to follow Rowan, that she'd brought him into the pack and mess, but Kellen's grip tightened slightly as if anticipating her refusal. She nodded slightly, praying Rowan was safe. If anything happened to him, Lyric would never forgive herself.

* * * *

Rowan's wolf was restless. Lying next to the woman he already knew owned him body and soul, he decided to stretch his legs and maybe let his wolf out. Knowing he was able to become a furry beast, and accepting the fact was becoming easier with each passing second.

He slid out of bed, admiring Lyric's naked form. His body responded to the sight of her luscious curves. The thought of sliding between her thighs and waking his mate back up almost had him doing just that, but a feeling something wasn't right made him dress in record time. Easing out into the hallway, he wished there was a way to bar the door, other than breaking the lock, but he didn't want to prevent Lyric from getting out in case of an emergency.

His wolf scratched at his mind, wanting to be let out. Rowan allowed the beast to surface, just enough to help him navigate the halls he'd never been in. The dimly lit walkways inclined as if they were leading back toward the surface a bit. He came to a halt outside a huge steel door where another state-of-the-art keypad was located. The camera showed him several men in camo searching around the surface near the entrance. Rage threatened to consume him at the thought of them breaking into the safe house where he and his mate were sleeping.

He punched in the code Lyric had used to access the other door, unimpressed when the thick door's bolts could be heard unlocking. His wolf's hearing picked up the men above moving down the hidden entrance toward him. Making sure he locked the door behind him, Rowan let more of his beast out, preparing to meet them. He'd protect what was his, and the people behind him were his, especially Lyric, his mate.

"Hello, boys. Can I help you?" he asked, his voice more gravelly with the wolf half of him taking up residence.

Four men skidded to a halt on the wet leaves, their camo proving they'd planned to blend into the foliage.

"We only want to talk to the leader." One of the men held a black nightstick, tapping it against his thigh.

Rowan grunted. "And you thought sneaking around in the dark would get you an audience with the alpha, much less would get you a sit down that didn't include him beating your ass?" Rowan kept to the shadows, knowing they couldn't see his face or the fact he'd partially shifted. He couldn't scent shifter on any of them, not like he could when he'd first met Lyric's pack.

"We were told if we proved ourselves, they'd allow us to become one of them." A younger man said hesitantly.

The man with the long rod knocked it against his thigh, and a crackling sound reached Rowan's ears. With speed, he struck the man closest to him in the throat, lifting him into his arms and launching him at the man with the nightstick. The youngest of the group saw what was clearly the leaders go down and reached for his own Taser. Hating to hurt the young man, Rowan backhanded him. He felt a shock hit him in the back and twisted to see the last man standing, a look of triumph on his face. Rowan ripped the prongs out of his back, pulling the man to him. The man began to struggle, jerking a knife from his belt faster than Rowan had expected.

"I thought this was supposed to be a...gathering intel mission," he spat. "But, it's you or me, asshole." The knife swung in a wide arc, slicing into Rowan's chest. The burn left in its wake was minimal, enraging more than anything.

"Ah, little man, they should've sent more than

pups in after the big boys," Rowan taunted, letting the man see his contorted face for the first time. "Now, you will take me to the men who sent you."

The faint scent of urine hit Rowan's nostrils. "What are you?"

Rowan grabbed the zip ties from the man's belt, shaking his head at the absurdity, and tied him up. He then checked for a pulse on the two unconscious men and the youngest one who couldn't be more than a teen.

"How did you get recruited?" Rowan asked.

When the only conscious one didn't answer, he squatted down and looked him in the eyes, pulling his wolf back so he faced him as a man. "Listen, I didn't know anything about shifters until I was attacked outside a bar a couple of nights ago. I think the men who sent you after me are the ones who did it. If we work together, maybe we can stop another from being hurt, or worse, killed."

His voice shook. "You aren't going to kill me?"

Rowan took a deep breath, wishing he didn't have to smell the man's piss, but no scent of lies permeated the air. He'd been good at telling if someone was lying before he'd been changed, now he had an added helper. "As long as you tell me the truth and don't try to hurt those I care for? No."

With a jerk of his head, the younger man nodded. Rowan slung two bodies over one shoulder, the other he dragged up the incline, shaking at the knowledge they'd come so close to where he'd been sleeping with Lyric.

At the top, he looked back and forth, waiting for the kid to indicate which way they'd left their vehicle.

. "I can't remember which way we came."

His heightened senses smelled no untruth. The men shifted in his arms, and Rowan made a snap decision. He'd picked up their Tasers and shoved them into the waistband of his pants. Dropping them, he tasered first one and then the others, making sure none would wake up. Signs of the men's trek were visible to him as he looked closer. Rowan wasn't sure if they were amateurs or if it was all a setup. The men from the bar were much more organized and a lot tougher than the four he'd faced here. He looked at the kid again, a growl rising in his chest. "Boy, you'd better start being straight with me or I'll rip your fucking throat out and shit down your neck." His beast pushed to the front, needing to protect what was his.

"We were told where to find this hidden place.

Our job was just to come and see if it was really here. You shocked us all when you came out of there."

No change in his scent. Either the guy was a good liar or he was telling the truth. A sudden rush of power washed over him, making him smile. Kellen wasn't one for subtlety, although Rowan didn't hear the other man until he was almost on top of them. Something not many people could do.

"What's doin boys?" Kellen's deep rumble filled the night air. The young kid dropped to his knees. Even non-shifters couldn't fight an alpha's power.

Kellen's right brow lifted as Rowan stood his ground. "I felt something was off and went to investigate. What I found was these yahoos." Rowan explained what had happened after he'd opened the door. Had the men he'd tasered still been conscious, Kellen would have probably beat them down. His fingernails lengthened to deadly black claws, igniting fear in the only man who could give the answers they needed.

"What's your name, and if you lie, or do anything I don't like, I will cut you." Kellen brought his claws up for him to see.

Audibly swallowing, sweat dripping down his brow, he opened his mouth then shut it.

"You think I won't?" Kellen lifted his arm that had shifted into more wolf than man.

"They weren't lying. You're really a wolfman?"

"Oh, yeah. Wanna see how big my teeth are?" Kellen smiled, flashing fangs much larger than humans'.

"Mike. My name is Mike. I thought this was a recon, not a capture or whatever, man. I swear. I didn't sign up for this, and they promised us backup."

"Who promised you these things, Mike?" Kellen asked, his wolf back under the skin. Rowan was impressed with how easily the alpha shifted seamlessly.

"My fraternity."

Rowan looked at the downed men and then at Mike. "That doesn't make sense, Kellen. This kid looks young enough, but these guys..." he said, thinking about waking one of them. "They are too old to be in college."

"Listen you little fuck, I'm done playing games. Do you know you can live without a dick? They'll call you a eunuch, or a chick, but I don't give two fucks what you're called. Last chance." Kellen grabbed the kid by the throat, easily lifting him off the ground.

Rowan's ears picked up the sound of

approaching men. His body stilled as he half shifted. "Kellen we got company coming at us from the east."

"That would be Xan and the boys."

He wondered how Kellen knew but assumed it had to do with their sense of smell. Yeah, he was still getting used to the whole wolf thing.

"Please tell me you aren't swinging for our team now, Alpha." Xan came up like a silent wraith. Rowan was sure he was with the men he'd heard coming from the east, only he spoke right next to the downed men, coming out of the woods from the west.

"When I drop this kid, I'll shove something up your ass if you want, Xan." There was no heat to either of their words, letting Rowan know they joked with each other all the time.

"Guys, I really don't want anything up my ass. I'm sorry I came here. I swear it. I don't know what's real or fake. I feel like pieces are missing."

Truth. Rowan could hear it and wasn't sure what to make of it.

"The guys who tried to take Lyric were very organized. I'd say they had the ability to wash these guys. That's what this seems like to me." He stopped at the questioning looks on the men's faces. "That means they are dispensable."

"Ah, shit. You're military. Have you seen this before?" Xan asked, and pulled up the larger man who had started to wake. "I think you killed this one."

"Coti, did you go to medical school?" Kellen asked.

"Does fucking a chick while she was in nursing school count?"

Xan punched the man named Coti. "If it worked that way, I'd be every fucking profession known to man, and some that haven't even been created yet."

The bald man had a few inches on both the alpha and Xan, yet he tilted his head as if thinking. "So you're saying you are a manwhore."

"I'm saying you're a dumbass. However, I won't deny having my fair share of women."

"Can we get back to the matter at hand, children? Namely, who wants to kill the boy here for lying to me? I've met my quota for the week, and I've got two women waiting on me back at my place. I don't need blood on my hands when I slide between them." Kellen held the young man out as if in offering.

"Fine, give him to me. I'll do it." Coti held his hand out. Rowan wondered if they were seriously going to kill the kid and the other guys. He'd skated the line in the military, but here at home, he wasn't sure he could turn a blind eye. Insta-wolf didn't make him lose his values.

"Alpha, I found their vehicle. They've got a tracker, too."

"Good job, Wyck."

Rowan was having a hard time keeping track of all the men coming out of the woods. He hadn't even sensed the huge African American man Kellen called Wyck. His ghost team would kick him out without a backward glance.

"Don't beat yourself up, bro. Nobody can hear Wyck except for the alpha," Coti explained. "Am I killing the kid or what? I need pussy, and I don't see any here, so let's get this done." The man shook his head, and, in moments he'd shifted to the thing of nightmares. Half man, half wolf.

"Fuck, I hate when he does that. You know that's what they based the movie *An American Werewolf in London* off of right?" Wyck crossed his arms over his chest.

Kellen growled. "Coti, you got babysitting duty for the kid. Wyck carry the douche nozzles back to their vehicles. Let's see what happens when they get back inside. Any word on Taya?"

"Wait. There was a woman. I remember a

woman with long red hair and tattoos. They had her chained to a bed. I asked about her, but the boss said she was into BDSM and not to worry about it. Only she looked scared and her screams didn't sound like one of pleasure."

Like this kid knew anything about giving a woman pleasure.

At his words Xan knocked the boy out of Kellen's hands, falling to the ground with a thud. The ferocity of the act startled the alpha so much, he fell on his back as Xan wrapped his hands around the throat of the kid.

Rowan feared his mate's brother would kill him before they could find out what the hell was going on. Who Taya was to Xan was a mystery to him as well. Shit, this was a clusterfuck. He needed his own team that he trusted.

A big hand landed on his shoulder. "You can trust us. I know this is a lot to take in, but we are your family now." Wyck nodded toward the men on the ground.

Kellen grunted then jerked Xan up and off the kid. "We need him alive, jack-off."

"If he knows where Taya is then I'll beat it out of him." Xan's voice sounded more wolf than human.

"If you kill the little fucker, he won't be able to tell us shit, so get control, or I will." Kellen's power lashed out—even Rowan turned his neck along with Xan. The other wolves dropped down to one knee until Kellen pulled back.

"Fuck me running. I hate when you do that shit, man," Wyck complained.

"Taya's not my mate, so get that outta your head. She's seeing a dude whose family isn't all that accepting of her. I was just an ear these last few months. Yes, I've fucked her a few times, but it's been a very long time. Now, let's move this circus along." Xan brushed the dirt and leaves off his clothes.

"I know where the house is. I'll show you," Mike said.

"Kid, you tell us, and we will go there. If you're screwing around, I'll let Coti kill you slowly." Kellen spoke as if he was saying the sky was blue.

With chattering teeth, the young man held out his hands. "I only know how to get there, not how to tell you how to get there. I mean, that doesn't make sense, but I can see it in my head, I just can't...I don't know how to tell you."

Kellen looked up through the towering trees, looking for what? Rowan wasn't sure, but he wished they'd figure this out because he wanted to get back to his mate.

Chapter Six

Lyric had moved past worried to freak the fuck out. She'd expected someone to come back and tell her all was okay. Or have her mate come sauntering through the door so she could kick his ass and then kiss his boo boo. As the minutes turned to a half hour and then an hour, she became even more worried. Their location had been compromised, and her mate was out there bleeding.

She thought about calling out to Kellen, or her brother Xan, but fear for their safety if they were in the middle of a battle kept her in check. Knowing her friends were locked up in their own safe spots, she had nothing better to do than pace back and forth. Rowan's scent still clinging to her body made her ache for him.

Mr. McCartney eyed her with a look she couldn't decipher. His wife sat behind him, chewing on her thumbnail.

Several of the high-ranking wolves had taken up residence in the lower levels under the club. She could see the McCartney's didn't care to have that

much testosterone in one space without their
attention directed elsewhere. All unmated females
had been accounted for, except for Taya, and steps
taken to ensure the weaker were safe until the threat
was taken care of. So why then was Lyric feeling as if
something was off in one of the safest places?

A look around at all the familiar faces didn't turn
up anything out of place. Her wolf itched to get out
and protect her. Lyric had learned early on to listen
to the other half of herself, and allowed a partial shift,
one that would go unnoticed. Her brown eyes became
those of the wolf, and beneath her blonde hair she
allowed her ears to shift along with her nails. The
men may be a lot bigger and stronger, but she was
faster and smarter. If there was a threat amongst
them, she would not be an easy target.

Her ears twitched at the sound of static coming
from the office of the older couple. The noise
reminded her of the walkie talkies she and Syn had
played with as children. Why they would have such
archaic devices, Lyric had no clue.

Not wanting to alert them to her plans, but
needing to find out if they had betrayed the pack,
Lyric entered their space. The static was even louder
now that she was in there. Most of the wolves had no

reason to enter where the McCartney's spent their time, and Lyric could count on one hand the occasions she'd come inside. The sound came from Mrs. McCartney's purse. Lyric looked around, hating to snoop through another woman's personal belongings, but saw no way around it. As she stood there contemplating what to do, she noticed several other disturbing things. A picture of a man who looked very similar to one of the men who had attacked her outside of the club, was tucked away in the corner, almost hidden. Any bit of guilt evaporated. Knocking over the plaid bag, and watching the contents spill out, Lyric bent to pick it back up.

The walkie talkie had been turned down too low for most to hear. With a small adjustment, the device beeped, and then a man's voice came across.

"We are five minutes out. How many are there? Just push the button if you can't speak with the number."

Anger threatened to overwhelm her good sense. They had five minutes to get out or prepare to defend themselves against an attack against who knew how many. In the tunnels, they were sitting ducks, but if they got back up to the club, they at least had a fighting chance.

Grabbing the little black walkie talkie, Lyric stepped out of the office. Arynn the omega was there along with Bodhi the beta. She walked up to the beta, and, in as few words as possible told him in a whisper, too low for the others to hear. The immediate change in Bodhi had her stepping back.

"You two, over here now." Bodhi pointed at the McCartney's.

The other pack members formed a band around them, making sure the elder couple couldn't escape. They didn't need to know why Bodhi was ordering them to him, only that he'd taken the place of Kellen in his absence.

Mr. McCartney was the first to comply, while his wife's face contorted into one of loathing. "You and your filth use this pack and this club like a whorehouse with a swinging door. Your alpha is a sadist who takes pleasure in hurting the females of the pack, and yet they can't wait to come crawling back. I would never allow my family to become part of such depravity, and when my nephew and his pack wipe the likes of you from here, I'll be revered, instead of used as a gatekeeper of a whorehouse," Mrs. McCartney spat.

The depth of her hate resounded around the space.

"The man on the other end said they were five minutes out about a minute ago. We're sitting ducks down here, not knowing how many he's bringing, especially not knowing where he'll come at us. I suggest we go up to the club, and change the master lock key code. Kellen can still override it, but I'm assuming they gave their nephew access. If we change it now, it may buy us a few extra minutes." Bodhi's voice came out more like a growl.

Arynn nodded before taking off at a jog toward the computer room.

"Since I don't have the authority to kill you, yet, you are both coming with us, but I do have the right to do this," Bodhi said, knocking Mr. McCartney unconscious in one swift move. The look he gave Mrs. McCartney said he'd like to do a lot worse to her. The older woman's scent had changed from defiance to fear the moment Lyric had produced her way of contacting the other pack. It increased even more at the hate coming off of Bodhi.

Lyric stepped up to the older woman. "You've betrayed the pack and will be sentenced as such. You know Kellen will not let you go just because you are a woman and an elder. Bodhi is clearly too much of a gentlemen to do it, but I don't share his problem." With a flash of her fangs, Lyric hauled her arm back and punched the older woman.

"Damn, girl, I knew I loved you." Bodhi eyed her up and down. "Too bad you done mated another. Now, let's head up. Time's a-ticking. Bring the traitors with and tie them up; use extreme force."

"Kellen and the boys are on their way back. Bad news, their time frame is longer than five minutes. They were taken on a wild goose chase, it seems." Arynn growled. Being the omega, he could communicate with all the members without disrupting them because he was attuned to their well-being.

Lyric grabbed his hand. "Is Rowan okay?"

"Oh, your mate is fine. Pissed beyond belief, but fine."

Dread coiled within her as she pounded up the walkway back to the club. No doubt they'd be facing an army of wolves out for blood, whether they were ready or not. Fear was like a knot in the pit of her stomach. The other wolves took up places in front and behind her, acting as protectors.

Bodhi's face could've been carved in stone.

"Don't even think to move from the spot we put you. If I tell you to stay put, you stay put. If I say jump...." He raised his eyebrow.

"I'll say, how high," she answered.

He took a step closer, handsome features darkening as his body towered over her. "No, you will already be jumping. I say this not to be an overbearing ass, but because it could be the difference between life and death. Kellen and Xan have entrusted me with your life, and now your mate has done the same. I will see to your safety, and you will do as I say."

She swallowed what she worried was the beginning of a sob. All these wolves would give their lives before they allowed anything to happen to her. "Bodhi, I will hide in a box if it means I am not a distraction. I promise you this, though. I am a fighter. Both Kellen and my brother made sure Syn and I could fight off an amorous wolf."

Arynn's voice interrupted them. "The codes are changed." He looked around the large bar. "Every exit has been blocked, which means they have to come at us from the front. Or we will know when they breach the inner sanctum."

The tables were bolted down for the occasional—

or frequent—brawl. While they waited, the guys gathered the chairs and stacked them against the walls, clearing the space for the upcoming battle. Several men had already shifted, using their heightened senses.

Lyric shifted from one foot to the other. Hesitation and concern increasing her worry for all their safety. Most of the men who'd been called in were unmated and had vowed to always put pack first. What had happened in the first place that could cause an all-out war?

"Should I shift?" she asked gravely.

Bodhi frowned at her; his need to take action burned through his gaze. "It doesn't matter what form you take, you will be no match for a dominate wolf, chérie."

The usual pain knifed through her, but she wouldn't allow it to defeat her purpose. They had never seen her in action. She and Syn were always treated as cosseted princesses, so his words didn't surprise her. She lifted her chin. "Tell me what you want me to do and then go do your thing. I can and will fight, Bodhi. Surely they will be beating down the doors any minute."

A muscle twitched in his jaw, a sure sign he

didn't like her words or her actions. "Go behind the bar. If they make it through the front line, you get into the safest position you can, and you do your damndest to stay alive. You hear me?"

"I hear you." she snapped.

His voice dropped to a low timbre. "I lost my baby sister years ago. I won't let that happen to Xan's if I can help it."

Though her heart ached for his loved one, Lyric wouldn't stand back and allow the men to die while she hid in fear. His eyes held the misery of years, and she silently vowed to stand her ground.

Thunder rumbled outside, almost drowning out the noise of incoming feet. Flashes of lightening lit up the windows, allowing the shadows of their enemies to be seen for seconds at a time.

Everyone inside the club took up position, watching the silent figures slither closer. Not a soul dared breath. They had enemies coming from two sides. If her nose was correct, over fifteen shifters approached, ten from the front, five in the tunnels. They were outnumbered.

She saw what Turo, one of the bartenders, called the equalizer, strapped under the counter. He'd probably want to beat her ass when he learned she used his precious AR-15, what the hell ever it was, but Lyric could give two shits. All she cared about in that moment, was that he always kept a full magazine in it, and Turo said that it was thirty percent more accurate than his AK-47. The lightness of the weapon almost caused her to drop it. She'd been shooting rifles for years and felt secure that her aim was good enough.

When the first door collapsed under the barrage of wolves, chaos reigned like the storm outside. Like the hounds of Hell they were, spittle falling from their jaws, they attacked en masse.

Lyric sat with her back to the wall. Her one glance around the corner had sent her scuttling back with her borrowed gun in her lap, and she felt like a coward. The sound of growls and battle was louder than the booming thunder outside, drowning out the sound of her beating heart.

A crash alerted her to the front door breaking down; the scent of moisture blowing in with the wind combined with the stench of their enemies. Her body jerked with each of her pack members' howls. Alerted by murmurs of approaching wolves coming around the bar, she tucked herself into a tight ball, inwardly cursing her cowardice.

One hand clasped the gun while she peered out of the small space. Not two feet from her was a mangy wolf that looked diseased. His yellow eyes rotated this way and that, before he lifted his lips in a snarl, distracted by the smell of liquor. Behind him, another wolf looking just the same nudged him, swiping at his side with claws not quite as deadly as her own. The biggest challenge was shooting the gun in a half shift.

Eventually, they moved away, returning as if they sensed something was amiss. Taking a deep breath, Lyric made sure the gun was ready to fire.

The sound of howls and growls increased.

Even through the mayhem, the two wolves now stalking her weren't deterred from their search. It was as if they'd been given her scent. A knife came sailing by, impaling the wolf closest to her. He jerked, and his fetid breath reached where she sat. Turo stomped past, coming from the opposite direction, twisting the downed wolf in one beefy arm before jerking his knife out of the carcass. The other wolf reared back on his hind legs as Turo motioned him forward, his big body between her and the wolves. He grunted as the deranged wolf attacked, the small claws leaving a trail of blood across his forearm. And still she kept to her corner and stayed motionless and quiet.

"You stay down and keep my baby safe. Fire at anything that looks like those fuckers. However, I'm gonna have your brother buy me the next box of bullets." His gravelly voice was barely above a whisper.

Turo leapt over the counter in one smooth move. Whatever had drawn his attention howled in pain and then went silent.

The sound of large claws clacking against the cement flooring had her swiveling to the left. She raked her gaze from the black claws of a male wolf up to the towering face of pure evil. He was clearly an alpha with no sense of morality, and he knew exactly where she was. His eyes didn't skitter back and forth searching, just zeroed in on her hiding spot, she jerked back, hoping he didn't see her, but knew it was useless as the sound of his footfalls came closer.

Lyric jumped up, abandoning her sanctuary, with the AR-15 pointed straight at his chest, which was eye level with her head. Fuck, he was bigger than Kellen and Xan. Keeping her back to the wall, she looked expectantly off to the side.

No savior in sight.

Two more leapt over the bar, startling her. The gun wavered and then her will to live and fight kicked in. She smiled the same shit-eating grin that always got her in trouble, a look that set her brother's back teeth on edge. The big bad wolf snarled while his two minions scrabbled for purchase. Lifting the gun to her shoulder, she fired, her aim true. The kick knocked her off balance for a moment, a distraction that cost her leverage.

A rousing chorus of howls rent the air.

Her grip on the machine gun didn't ease, even as the larger wolf jumped on top of her, with the barrel pointing toward the wall, she eased off the trigger not wanting to accidentally hit one of her pack. His hatred for her was palpable. Blood dripped onto her from a wound in his side. She wanted to cheer at the damage she'd caused.

"You're a coward, wolf. You may be the alpha of your pack, but you will never be a real alpha. You can kill me, but what does that get you?" She spoke to the wolf, knowing he could hear and understand her. "I won't turn my neck. You don't deserve that distinction," she spat.

* * * *

Rowan's heart was threatening to burst out of his chest. The Iron Wolf Club looked like a scene straight out of a horror movie. The truck he'd been riding in hadn't come to a complete stop when he'd jumped out, the scent of death and blood assaulting his senses.

Seeing the doors ripped off, he and the other men ran through, some shifted, others half-shifted. Rowan searched for Lyric through the fighting. Kellen had told him to follow his nose. He wasn't sure what the other man meant until he'd come face to face with an onslaught of wolves he'd never met. Instinct and scent told him which were on their side.

He ducked as a wolf came sailing over his head. The lifeless body one of the enemies made him breathe easier.

Abrupt gunfire brought everyone to a grinding halt. The sound was one he was familiar with from his combat days, but wasn't sure who had fired the deadly weapon until the petite form of his mate was the only one near the sound still firing. She held the black gun, shooting at two large wolves as they charged her.

His eyes widened when another wolf, larger than

any he'd seen, leapt on top of her.

Rowan would kill the wolf. He shifted, uncaring of his clothes ripping. The brown wolf had Lyric caged beneath him while she taunted him. Oh, he was so gonna spank her, or bite her. The big gun looked ready to bend beneath the pressure of the wolf, a sinking feeling of being too late entered his mind. He wouldn't allow it. She'd saved him. It was his turn to save her. Then he'd bend her over his knee and spank her beautiful heart-shaped ass, after he made love to her.

His wolf pushed the human side of him back, snarling a warning at the larger wolf. With Xan coming at the wolf from behind, Lyric was in a very precarious position. He could see the metal giving, her strength no match for man or beast as she used the gun to keep the wolf from getting to her throat. And then she shocked him by shifting. The swiftness of the action startled the wolf, as well, allowing Lyric a chance to shimmy out from under him.

Lunging across the space, Rowan slammed into him head on. The gun went off, causing everyone to jump except Rowan. Blood oozed from wounds on the other wolf; he swung his head back and forth, looking for a way out. With Xan blocking one end and

Rowan the other, he had no chance of escape.

Rowan flicked his wolven tongue out and licked his fangs, taunting the other beast. His focus narrowed down to what the other would choose to do now that he was cornered. His opponent's hind legs shifted, a slight twist. A bullet had hit him in the left leg, making the leap over the bar almost impossible. He looked to be thinking of trying, and then turned toward Xan, barreling into Lyric's brother with all his might. The action was swift and vicious as he swiped a huge paw aimed to take out Xan's jugular, only his mate's brother was faster.

Xan's growl was chilling. He knocked the brown wolf to the side, but fell in the pool of blood.

Rowan glanced around to check on Lyric. Her wolf stood proud, shaking debris from broken bottles from her fur. Acceptance of what he had to do shone in her amber depths.

Stalking the beast that tried to kill his mate across the cement floor, Rowan snapped his teeth, growling out a challenge. A huge man, with tattoos on both arms, and two other men, equally as big blocked the door, grins on their faces that did not make them look any less menacing.

The brown wolf turned around, his gaze taking in

what was left of his crew. A howl of rage flew from him. Rowan's howl was louder.

Not knowing protocol on wolf fights, uncaring how they should go, Rowan charged the wolf. His injuries too severe, the brown wolf didn't put up much of a fight. The light of battle had already began to dim as Rowan locked his jaws around the other's throat. He took pleasure in ending the wolf's life, not repulsed by the blood in his mouth. His wolf shook its head back and forth, making sure the enemy wouldn't get up.

"You can let go now, my love." Lyric stood behind him, her face streaked with grime.

"You, little missy, owe me an AR-15. Do you know how much they cost?" Turo walked up holding the pieces of his gun.

Rowan wanted to smile, but, in his wolf form, found it didn't quite look the same.

"You scared of being naked in front of all these boys?" she asked, scratching his head.

Yeah, his woman was in so much trouble. He shifted, uncaring of his nudity.

"I'll get you the newest model." Rowan looked up at the man standing far too close.

"Rowan, this is Arturo, but he goes by Turo.

Turo, this is my mate." She shifted from foot to foot as she realized what she'd called him.

Her words caused his wolf to settle.

"Dude, put some clothes on. You're gonna make Xan jealous and shit." Kellen slapped him on the back, a pair of sweats landing at his feet. They obviously kept supplies of extra clothes everywhere. His shoes were trashed, but he'd walked over a lot worse.

"Pretty sure I ain't heard no complaints, bro. As a matter of fact—" he stopped laughing as Lyric tossed a piece of metal at him.

"If you value your manhood, I suggest you don't finish that." Lyric glared at him.

Turo nudged Xan aside. "Shut it. This guy was just explaining how he was replacing my baby."

The light that shone in the otherwise harsh face was almost comical.

"I can get you a replacement. No problem." Rowan waved away his concerns.

He recognized the woman with flowing black hair that would stop traffic in any major city strolling through the door. Her blue eyes reminded him of the clearest ocean. If he wasn't already head over ass in love with Lyric, he'd have fallen in lust at first sight.

As it was, his mate elbowed him in the side, a smile on her beautiful face. "That's my best friend, Karsyn Styles, Syn to her friends, trouble with a capital T to her brother, Kellen. Oh, and here it comes."

He was going to question what she meant, but her meaning became obvious in less than twenty seconds. All the wolves in the room stopped what they were doing, stood straight, and stared toward the entryway.

Kellen's shoulders stiffened, his hands flexed into tight fists. "Karsyn, did I tell you it was safe to leave?"

Syn flicked her long hair over her shoulder. "Kellen, did I ask you for your permission?" She drew his name out in a long drawl. "I don't believe I need to ask you if I may leave my home. The alarm was lifted, hence I'm here."

"She's itching for a fight," Lyric whispered.

Rowan had figured that out. Why, was the question?

Placing her hands on hips exposed by her barely there daisy dukes, Syn stared her brother down. Her gaze raked over him then around the room. Who she looked for, Rowan wasn't sure. Testosterone levels increased so much, his wolf itched to push Lyric

141

behind him. Several growls echoed around the otherwise quiet space.

"I came to tell you the police have heard of a disturbance. Luckily, I was dating the chief a couple weeks back, and he called to see if I was okay. You know how they hate coming this far outside the city. However, the sheriff's department doesn't have such an affliction."

At the mention of her dating, or whatever, the big man named Bodhi stomped out from behind the bar. "What the fuck do you mean, you were dating the chief?" he asked, his dark eyes blacker than the blackest night.

Syn shrugged. "Let's get this place cleaned up, if we plan to open any time soon." She didn't so much as walk, but sashay across the blood-and-dirt filled room, carefully stepping over bodies as if it were an everyday occurrence and she was the queen of the castle.

"Um, baby, do you dress like that?" He tilted his head in the direction the other woman had disappeared.

Lyric laughed. "I'm not sure where she found those shorts. I think they're from like ninth grade, but they got the response she was looking for."

"If you mean she has her brother ready to rip every man's head off and Bodhi's blood vessel in his right temple ready to explode, then, yes, mission accomplished."

They worked as a team cleaning up the mess left behind from the fight. He was surprised when the fallen wolves didn't shift back to men, until Kellen explained if you died in your shifted form then that was how you stayed. The biggest problem with that was they were unable to learn their identities, making the question of why they were attacked an unsolved issue.

"Did you find Taya?" Lyric asked as they loaded up into his big truck.

Rowan turned to look at the bar, a scowl on his face. "Yeah, she's a little worse for wear, but she'll recover."

Lyric shook her head. "Xan cares about her, but she's not his mate. I'm glad she's okay. She'll probably head back home to Mystic, South Dakota. That's where she's originally from."

"Is there another pack there?" Rowan asked, thinking he really needed to learn more.

"Yes. I don't know all the details, just that she has family there."

Rowan felt sorry for the other woman, but his first worry was for his own mate.

He wanted to get her back to his place and shower the stink of fighting and death off both of them before he made love to her. He'd heard the word mate bandied about, saw the flash of fear in Lyric's eyes every time. Rowan knew what it meant on some levels. His own mind had flashed the word to him earlier. His wolf wanted her and no other, and so did he. They both needed to let their woman know she was it for them. Mate. She was their mate. Their woman. His wolf settled as he accepted it.

Rowan laced his fingers through hers. They'd both washed their hands and faces, however, their clothes, and everything from their necks to their toes, were covered in dirt and grime.

When he pulled into the garage, Lyric's fingers loosened, but his tightened, pulling her across the seat and out his door. After the night he'd had, the fear of what could've happened to her, Rowan wasn't sure he could let Lyric out of his sight for the foreseeable future. She didn't seem to mind, wrapping her legs around his waist as he maneuvered them through his quiet home. His bare feet left traces of what they'd been through on the tile and wood.

How he'd explain the mess to his housekeeper, he
had no clue, nor did he care.

Ignoring the big bed that dominated his
bedroom, he carried his precious woman into his en
suite. The luxurious room was one he'd spared no
expense on.

"Do you like this outfit, darling?"

"Oh, fuck, no. Get it off me." Lyric locked her legs
around his waist, pulling her T-shirt off, trusting him
to hold her up.

The tiled shower drew him, but he could also
picture setting her on the double vanity with the
mirror behind it. The height would be perfect for him
to sit Lyric on the edge while he fucked her, or he
could bend her over and watch her expression in the
mirror as he pounded into her from behind.

"What has that look on your face?" Lyric bit at
his lower lip.

Rowan captured her mouth with his own, telling
her in explicit detail what he'd imagined doing to her.

"Holy fuck me running. You keep that shit up
and I'm liable to come in my panties."

A growl escaped at her words, and the smell of
her arousal let him know she was telling the truth.
Rowan used his strength to unlock her feet from

behind him, stripping the remaining clothes from both of them. "Why, you little liar. You don't have any panties on." He swatted her behind. The playful tap had the fleshy little cheek bouncing. A pink flush covered her face.

"Oopsie, I must have left them back at the clubhouse." She blinked over her shoulder at him, smiling playfully.

Damn, he loved her and her dirty mouth. "In you go." He watched her look at the large, decadent shower with the wide shelf built into one wall. When he'd had the blueprints drawn up, he'd had it designed with the sole purpose of sex in mind. The builder had raised his eyebrows, probably doing a little math and coming up with the exact height of Rowan, but he didn't care. He'd wanted to be able to set his wife on the ledge, and be at the perfect height to slide between her legs.

With a press of a few buttons, the multi-head showers came on, and he allowed a few minutes for the water to warm up before he settled Lyric in front of them. Taking the time to wash her and then himself nearly killed him. Her breathing had turned into little pants.

His mate was clean, and his dick twitched to be

inside her. He sat her on the platform, wedging his hips between her legs. Her pussy was right there, glistening with arousal all for him.

"Mate. I like it. No." He shook his head, water droplets flying. "I love that word. From what I know about wolves, that means life. Right?" His cock poised at her entrance. Her startled gasp had him smiling.

Chapter Seven

Lyric reached out and touched the rough jaw of her mate. He knew about their status. She inhaled and tested the air smelling nothing but truth. It felt wonderful to be able to brush her finger over his skin. The heat of longing rose in both of them, from their connection it increased her arousal.

A wondrous look came into his black eyes. She'd put that look there.

"You gonna do something with that big boy, or you just planning on teasing me?" She gestured toward the twitching dick between her thighs; her fingers brushed the head.

He crowded her, forcing her back against the wall. His dominance didn't scare Lyric. His cock nudged against her opening, pressing forward and then retreating. He seemed intent on torturing her slowly as he loomed over her, those midnight dark eyes of his staring down as his body took possession of her.

Their bodies welcomed each other, just as their wolves did. She could feel her wolf relaxing, that constant war, an itch to get out after a scary situation, needing a way to burn off the excess energy dissipating under Rowan's love.

"I love you, Rowan. You don't have to say it back. For wolves it's different than humans, but I have to say it or I'll explode." She couldn't stop the words from flowing out of her mouth any more than she could stop a hurricane.

Rowan's mouth dropped open as if he wasn't sure what to say or maybe her words had shocked him.

She shook her head, tears clogging her throat. "Please fuck me."

He pulled out, despite her tight grip around him. "Holy shit, woman. I'm head over ass in love with you." He punctuated each word with a slam of his cock into her.

She gasped, his actions were so swift and his words so startling she couldn't protest either of them. The sound of wet bodies slapping increased in tempo. Her eyes watered, ecstasy and happiness combined lighting every inch of her being and making her feel more alive than ever. She wasn't sure where she began and he ended, but one thing she did know, he was it for her.

He took control as her orgasm washed over her, his mouth latched onto her nipple, making her arch into him. The water pounded around them, but she felt positively sheltered from it, surrounded by him as she was. When he licked her nipple then bit down on the tender flesh, Lyric swore she saw stars behind her closed eyelids, like he knew just what to do to make her body come alive for him.

Holding onto control by a thread, she wanted to feel him coming with her. She pried her eyes open, feeling him swell deep within her as his movements never ceased. His hips slammed back and forth, swiveling, pressing her against the tile, making Lyric feel helpless and small yet protected from the world.

When he switched to the other breast, giving it the same attention as the first, she gave up, mini quakes shaking her body. She locked her legs around his waist holding on for all that she was worth.

His big cock pounded inside her, and then he was kissing her. Lips and tongue plundering. She couldn't get enough of him, couldn't imagine a time she ever would. She slid her tongue along his, wrapped her arms around his neck as he moved his finger down her stomach.

"You're so tight, so hot. I want to feel you come

around me. Come with me."

Trapped between the man she loved and the tile wall, she finally felt like she was home. Lyric had found a mate, an accidental mate who loved her and made her feel safe.

Rowan covered her from head to toe, seated to the hilt, he pulled back and thrust back in. Over and over again. His cock rubbed the G-spot inside while his finger brushed her clit. He had her ready, body primed, and her orgasm threatening to go off any moment.

"With you. I want to come with you," she panted.

His mouth came down on hers again, his tongue seeking entrance, fucking into her mouth in the same rhythm as their bodies. His hands on the cheeks of her ass were almost bruising, forcing her to ride the beat he set up.

Lyric's nails bit into his shoulders as the pressure built, and finally he pushed her over the edge.

Rowan released her lips, roaring out his own release. She felt his cock stretching her, his semen spilling inside her, and still he stayed seated deep within long after the last of his come had left his body, shudders racking them both.

His hands stroked over her body. "Did I hurt

you?"

She felt pleasantly sore and a little weak from exhaustion, but hurt was the last thing she was. "I'm pretty sure I left deep scratches on you, babe." Her pussy did feel a little stretched but eager for more. Her hand lifted to run across his scalp, she watched his eyes close like a domesticated kitten. She laughed.

"Why are you laughing?" he mock growled.

"I just thought you looked like a sweet kitten."

Rowan hummed. "Well, I do like to lick cream." His tongue came out.

Lyric giggled, then whispered his name when he dropped to his knees, placing both of her feet on his shoulders, and proceeded to show her his version of what a kitten would do.

Lying in his large bed, Lyric thought about her best friend, Syn. Their plans had been carefully laid out until Rowan had come barreling in, or out as was the case, the bar door. She wondered what her friend was doing and if she was truly okay with Lyric's recently mated status.

Rowan stirred, his head rising from her chest. "I must not have done a very good job if you're awake before me."

A smile curved her lips. The man had more

stamina than a teenage boy. "Trust me, my love, you will hear no complaints from me."

He stroked his palm down her arm. "Then what has put those frown lines on your forehead?"

She wrinkled her nose at his description. "Puh-lease, don't tell me I'm getting wrinkles. I was just thinking about Syn."

Her mate snickered. "Again, I must not be doing a very good job if you're thinking about someone else in my bed."

Hiding a smile behind her hand, Lyric ran her thigh up Rowan's. "Wow, does someone need a little convincing he's all that and a bag of chips?"

Rowan huffed and rolled to his back, his dick hard as a spike, almost touching his belly button. "It's not me who needs convincing."

Lyric knelt, grasping his dick. "Oh, really. Who needs *convincing*?"

"He does." Rowan nodded at his cock.

She couldn't help it; she laughed out loud.

"Hey, it's not my fault. You know most men have two brains. This one and that one." He pointed at his head and then gripped his hand over hers, showing her the pressure he liked. "However, now I have a wolf inside me. I guess that means I have three."

Lyric had a feeling Rowan was going to use his manly attributes to his advantage, and she couldn't wait. She let him lead her hand up and down his shaft, loving how relaxed she was with him already. A drop of pearly fluid beaded on the tip. As she bent to taste his essence, he gripped her hair in his hand and held it back. She turned to watch him while she swiped her tongue across the mushroom-shaped head. His flavor burst across her tongue.

"Mmmm, breakfast in bed." Lyric licked him.

"Flip around, and we can both enjoy a little snack."

Her stomach flipped.

"I've never done that." She looked up at Rowan.

* * * *

Rowan could smell her arousal, loved it, and wanted to smell it every day for the rest of his life. He helped her maneuver over him, her perfect pussy pink and wet, her cream dripping down her thighs. He swiped his tongue up her inner leg, capturing as much as he could before moving up to lick at her pussy. His sweet mate took him into her mouth, trying to make him blow, but he was made of sterner

155

stuff.

He let his tongue trace circles around her labia, loving the unique flavor. Her tight cunt constricted as he fucked her with his mouth, her little mewling moans egging him on. He used his thumbs to hold her open, swiping back and forth, licking at her clit in quick yet not quite satisfying motions. Her cries and pleas went straight to his cock.

He'd planned to play with her, to extend their play, however Lyric had other plans. She used her mouth and hands, twisting them in tight fists, taking him to the root, all the way to the soft part at the back of her throat and swallowing.

He pulled her farther down onto his face, spreading her thighs wider so he could fuck his tongue up into her, his chin brushing her clit, sending her hips moving against his face. He pushed her up, dragged the flat of his tongue across her engorged clit, and pressed his thumb against her back hole, pressing down and stimulating the nerves back there.

She was on the edge, her thighs quivering.

He licked her from clit to ass, rubbing his thumb across her anus, knowing she'd never had a man there either, sucking one labia into his mouth and then the other. Pressing one then two fingers into her pussy, curving them up and finding her special spot. He pulled her clit into his mouth, felt the first pulse of her orgasm strum through her, and fucked and sucked until he felt the last twitch of her body. When she stopped squirming against his tongue, face, and fingers, he was surrounded by Lyric. Her taste, her scent, and her body.

His cock was ready to burst, but he was fine with it. His mate, on the other hand, was not.

"Oh, I think you have a boo boo," his mate murmured, and a gush of air blew across the tip of his dick. He hadn't even realized she'd released him.

He was ready to come within seconds of her tongue playing with his cockhead. There were no light sucking passes. No, his mate took him straight to the back of her throat and swallowed, her hands balanced on his thick thighs. He couldn't help but rub his nose in her pussy.

Over and over, she bobbed on his dick, using her tongue like she would if she were riding his cock, fucking him with her mouth. She sucked him down again, and all coherent thought fled his brain.

"Shit, I'm going to..."

Her hand tightened on him, the other gripped his balls. Any chance of pulling out evaporated. Lyric milked him of his seed, drinking him down and then licking him clean.

He felt utterly spent.

Lyric climbed off him, twisting until her head lay on his chest. "Best breakfast, ever."

He pressed a kiss to the top of her head and then heard her stomach growl. "Come on. I think I can whip us up something else to eat."

She made him weak in the best way possible. As he watched her get up and saw her wince, he knew he hadn't been the tenderest of lovers, but he didn't regret one moment. He'd just take extra care with her today, and tonight. The sparkle in her eyes as she turned to look at him had him hard all over again. "If you don't quit looking at me like that, I'll have your ass lubed up and take you there."

"I'm going to take a quick shower and meet you in the kitchen in five." She held up her hand.

Heat lit up her features; arousal filled the air. It took everything in him to slip on a pair of sweats and leave Lyric in his bedroom.

Seated at his state-of-the-art kitchen counter was Syn. He looked around, wondering how his mate's best friend had gotten into his home. The gorgeous woman wore a much more appropriate outfit than she'd had on the night before. Her shapely legs were crossed Indian style on the barstool as she watched him stroll into the room.

"Thank God. I thought you two were gonna fuck like bunnies for days or some shit." She held a paper cup from one of the local coffee shops in her hand. He couldn't believe he hadn't smelled the fresh brew.

"How the hell did you get in?" Rowan pulled the fridge door open. If the woman was there to kill him, he figured she'd already have done it.

Syn sniffed. "Puh-lease, you think your little alarm system could keep one such as I out."

Whatever else he would have said or asked was lost beneath the feminine squeals. He wasn't sure if he was ready for whatever trouble his mate and Syn had up their sleeves. The image of the huge man named Bodhi popped into his head. He was a newly mated male after all. Didn't he deserve a honeymoon or some shit?

"I so don't like that look, Mr. Shade," Lyric said.

Syn clapped. "Oh my gawd. We can totally say and mean it while crowd surfing, *Hey, we're throwing Shade.*"

A roaring started in his ears. "There will be no crowd surfing, mate."

Lyric patted his head. "Yes, dear."

Rowan grabbed Lyric around the waist, nibbling her neck where he'd marked her. "There will be no more accidents where you're concerned, if I have anything to say about it."

The End

Xan's Feisty Mate

Iron Wolves MC
Elle Boon

Chapter One

Brielyn Mattice, or Breezy to her friends, worked the kinks out of her shoulders after a long day in the ER. Lord, how she loved her job, but hated some of the doctors on staff. She grimaced as she thought about the newest fuck who thought he was god's gift to women. Sure, he was gorgeous with a great body and a good job, but that did not make him a good catch in her mind.

"Hey girl, you going to come out with us tonight?" Cheyenne asked, slamming her locker door shut.

The other nurse had already changed into a cute outfit ready to party, but Breezy just wanted to go home and soak in a hot bubble bath. "Nah, I think I'll just go home and read a book."

Her friend snorted. "What has happened to my cool friend? You know the one who was up for body shots and partying all night with me?"

It was her turn to snort. "First of all, the body shots were you, girlfriend. I just held your hair when you tossed your cookies later. You're welcome by the way. Second, I don't think I ever partied all night."

Cheyenne shrugged her shoulders. "I told Dr. Hottie you'd be there. He wouldn't agree to come if you weren't. Please come. You can leave after one drink."

Big brown eyes pleaded down at her, but Breezy wouldn't be swayed. She'd seen the way the doctor had looked at her and didn't want any part of him or any man for that matter. Well, no man other than the one who thought she was nothing better than a whore. If only he knew...she stopped her thoughts from swaying to the asshat who didn't deserve her, and focused on Cheyenne. "I promised my dad I'd pick up some dinner and bring it home. Sorry girl." She put just enough sorrow into her tone the other woman seemed to believe her. "Tell him I'm running late, and then pretend I texted you. Heck, I'll text you and say I changed my mind."

With a nod of her short dark head, Cheyenne

grabbed her bag and walked out of the locker room.

Breathing a sigh, she quickly changed, and then headed out shivering as she entered the parking garage. At eight o'clock in the evening, the lot was almost empty except for several cars she recognized as the late shift. She wished she would have parked closer to the elevator, but at the time there weren't any spots. Her shoes echoed through the concrete space, and she glanced around before reminding herself she was a wolf and could take care of herself.

Her vehicle was against the back wall, but with a feeling that wouldn't let up she looked around. The hair on the nape of her neck stood up. She reached into her bag for the can of Mace she kept there. A large arm grabbed her from behind pulling her between two parked cars, one gloved hand clamped over her mouth. Breezy froze in her attacker's arms, forgetting all the training her brothers and the Iron Wolves had taught her.

"I've got you now. Don't fight me and you won't get hurt...much," hot breath whispered in her ear.

She couldn't get any air inside her body with his large hand encased in leather gloves, covering both her mouth and nose. She began to feel lightheaded when her wolf woke up. Even though they all knew not to show their other half to humans, the fight or die instinct took over. Claws replaced her nails, and she dug them into her attackers thighs, her head went back. The satisfying sound of bone crunching had the man releasing his hold.

"You fucking cunt. I'll kill you."

Breezy gasped for air, her wolf wanting to lash out, but her human half still had control. She took a step away when his arm snaked out. Without thinking, she turned and hit him, getting her first glimpse of the masked man. He was large, almost as large as Xan. Fear and adrenalin kicked in. Her knee came up connecting with his family jewels, and at the same time he swung a right hook. She thanked the goddess her knee hit first, or knew his fist would have broken something. Stumbling back as he dropped to the ground, she didn't stop to think about her actions, just kicked him in the side of the head. Xan's words *to never let an opponent get back up or they'll stab you in the back* ringing in her head.

His groans and curses could be heard when she fled, but she didn't stop until she got to her car. Her hands shook so badly she dropped her keys, tears streaming down her cheeks, she swore it was like she was in a horror movie where the villain would jump up behind her at any moment. Finally, she unlocked her car with the press of a button and wasted no time backing out of the spot. Looking back, she saw the masked man standing at the end of the lot. The feel of her dinner threatening to come back up had her swallowing several times. The image of him doing the slow walk that all serial killers did as they caught up to their victims flashed before her eyes, making red dots appear and she realized she was holding her breath until she shot out of the enclosed garage.

"Oh, god. I almost died. Shit, shit, shit." She looked at the speedometer to see she was going way over the speed limit and laughed hysterically. "Having the police pull me over would be a bad thing how?" She looked in the rearview expecting to see a van or something following her. Once she was sure she wasn't being followed, she reached in her bag for her cell.

The thought of calling her dad and upsetting him was abhorrent to her, but she didn't have anyone else to call. Kellen was alpha of her pack and would always protect them, but she didn't want to make that call either. "It was probably just some random thing." After the incident with the McCartneys, she hated to bring her trouble to the pack. Remembering the size and feel of the man's hands on her, she dialed the clubhouse.

"Iron Wolves," Coti answered.

She breathed a sigh of relief. "Hey, Coti. It's Breezy." Her voice shook.

"What's the matter, nani?"

Breezy always sighed when he called her beautiful. People thought they'd make a great couple, but in reality, he was more like an older brother or best friend. She explained what had happened, and was about to say she was on her way home when the sound of rustling came over the line.

"Get your ass to the clubhouse, now, bella." Kellen's voice was low.

"I really want to go home and take a long bubble bath. I…"

Kellen cut her off. "That was not a request. If you don't want me showing up at your parents' home and dragging you out of there, I suggest you drive that fine ass here stat. I'm going to put Laikyn on the phone with you. I want you to talk with her until you get here. Do not hang up for any reason. Are you on a hands-free set?"

The need to salute him, and flip him off warred within her, but she also knew he was right. "Yes, I'm on my hands-free."

"Good. How far out are you?" His deep voice rumbled sending shivers through the phone line.

She didn't even think about denying him. "About fifteen minutes."

"Drive safe. And, bella, you were smart in calling."

Butterflies danced in her stomach.

****

Xander Carmichael or Xan to everyone, barely restrained his wolf. He'd been beta to the Iron Wolves since he'd turned twenty-five and he and Kellen had taken over, physically beating the fuck out of the old alpha and his worthless shits of leaders. They'd both been alphas in their own right, but Xan didn't want to lead. They opened the Iron Wolves MC shortly after and turned their little town back into a habitable place for wolves to live. Now, ten years later their families were all safe and well connected, albeit a little dysfunctional.

He couldn't imagine what sweet little Breezy was thinking. His wolf snorted. Yeah, she was far from sweet, but no woman deserved to be jumped in a parking lot, least of all one of their pack.

Violence. He was used to that emotion, and needed an outlet for what he was feeling. He turned to the back of the club. It was a Friday night, and the fights were just getting started. His pack and the MC held regular, no-holds-barred fights in the club. It wasn't often he had the urge to join in the cage, but when he did money tended to drop.

If he had any hope of facing Breezy with a semblance of control, he'd need to work out some of his anger, or he was liable to do something they'd both regret. Of course, he'd enjoy the fuck out of it and so would she, but he wasn't ready to mate any woman, even one as feisty as the delectable Breezy. When he finally did settle down, he didn't want one who'd been around the block like the town bicycle. Nope, he wanted a sweet woman who knew her place.

The sound of the loud bass met his ears long before he entered. Wyck looked him up and down as he walked in. "You fighting tonight?"

"Yep," he grunted.

Wyck smiled. The large African American slapped his hands together, the man was a blood thirsty bastard. Xan wondered if he was going to jump in the cage with him.

"I ain't got a death wish tonight." Brown eyes flashed at him as the bell rang signaling the end of the current fight. They didn't allow a fight to the death, but pretty damn close.

Tonight Xan had on a pair of worn denim jeans, and his customary black leather vest with the club insignia on the back. His black shitkickers were thick leather, but would come off before he entered the cage. He crossed to stand outside, watching as they carried out the unconscious man.

What a pussy, getting knocked out in the first five minutes.

He cracked his neck and waited to see if the winner planned to stay or leave. It wouldn't do to enter until the crowd was all riled up. With his arms crossed he stood, staring at the large male. Another shifter who was known for his bad attitude and even worse temper. Xan undid his boots, leaving them next to where he stood. His scent would deter anyone from taking them. The little wolf standing next to the door saw his approach, her eyes going wide. Xan couldn't remember her name, but when she held her hand out for his vest, he handed it over with a wink. "Take care, I'll be back for that shortly."

She blinked up at him, and at any other time he

might have bent and stole a kiss for luck. Instead he stood, gripped the cage door and swung up into the large square enclosure. There weren't too many rules when it came to fighting inside, except not to kill. Xan was down with that, everything else was open season.

He gestured to the other man, watching as Rocky, his name finally coming to Xan, danced around. The crowd noticed who'd entered, a hush fell over them.

"You ready for a beat down Club VP?" Rocky asked, hitting his chest.

Xan balanced on the balls of his feet. He wasn't going to waste his breath on the fuck. Again, he motioned Rocky forward, letting his lips kick up in a grin. His mama always said it was his shit-eating one that would piss off even the town priests. With a roar, Rocky lunged across the feet separating them. Xan side stepped, throwing his elbow out and hitting the back of the shifter's head, making him fall into the cage's steel links.

He ignored the crowd as they cheered. Rocky bounced back. They were both dirty fighters, and Xan prepared for the attack. Shifting to their wolves wasn't sanctioned since they allowed humans into the club, but speed and heightened strength was something they had in spades.

Again, Rocky charged him, going in low, his shoulder hit Xan in the mid-section while the man's fist pummeled at his kidney.

He tried to shake him off, but they fell to the ground, the feel of wolven claws digging into his side had Xan's wolf trying to surface. He growled. "What the fuck are you doing?"

Rocky's claws raked up his side. The thought the humans would see them, had his wolf snapping to be let out.

Xan rolled them, coming up on top, seeing hatred burning in Rocky's eyes, He rained blow after blow on the man, then when he realized Rocky wasn't fighting anymore he pulled back. His breathing hard, the sound of the cage door opening had him looking to see Kellen entering.

"You calm, bro?" Kellen nodded at the bloody beast beneath him.

The four long gashes down his side looked like Freddy Kruger had gotten a hold of him, ruining his favorite pair of jeans. "I'm level. This jackhole tried to shift in the middle of our fight. What the hell?" He kept his voice too low for anyone other than him and

Kellen to hear.

Kellen came over and inspected Rocky, felt the flutter of the man's heart and sat back on his heels. "At least he's still alive. I'd have killed the bastard."

A mirthless laugh escaped Xan. "I almost did. What brought you down to the cage?"

Kellen looked to the door of the club. "A swell in power and your girl is here. Thought you might want to come and see how she was doing for yourself. Of course, now it looks like she might need to patch you up."

In the doorway he saw a gorgeous vision of blonde hair with pink and purple streaks standing in a pair of jeans, looking like she'd painted them on, and a tank top that was snug enough he could make out the lace indents of her bra. For fucksake he felt his cock swell, and he was literally kneeling over a bleeding wolf. "Shit, she's not my woman, and I don't need her to patch me up."

His alpha snorted. "Right." The one word was drawled out.

Kellen snapped his fingers and a couple of the lower ranking wolves climbed into the cage. He listened with half an ear as they were instructed to take Rocky out, get him medical care and then he was to be placed in the detention center. Shite, Xan knew Kellen was pissed, but even he didn't think about the repercussions of the fight. Ever since the attack on Lyric and Taya, Kellen was tightening security and had become one hard-ass alpha. Not that he hadn't been before, but now you did not want to cross the man.

He thought back to the night his sister Lyric had been attacked outside a human bar. If it hadn't been for Rowan, an ex-special forces, he was sure she'd have been taken and possibly killed. Another member of the pack, Taya, had been taken and suffered much at the rogue pack's hands. Lyric had to turn the human Rowan in order to save him, and for that he was grateful since they were now happily mated. That didn't mean he believed in happily ever afters, it just meant Rowan got a reprieve from the beat down, until he fucked up and made his baby sister cry.

"Come on, I think the crowd has seen enough blood for the night." Kellen stood, his voice boomed out making the noise die down. "All right you dirty bastards, and sexy bitches. Next round is on the house, but don't get greedy. My staff knows what you normally drink, so don't piss me off." Warning given, he sauntered out.

The little wolf he'd given his vest to stood with an expectant look on her face.

"Thanks, sweets." He kissed her on the forehead, inhaling the smell of her shampoo and the scents of perfume and hair spray. He preferred the fresh smell of...he cut off the line of thought before it went any further, ignoring her practiced pout. His boots were where he'd left them. Not taking the time to shove his feet back into them, he made a beeline for the place he'd seen Breezy last. He promised himself he wouldn't threaten to rip off Coti's arms if he found them together. It would be better for all of them if the two would mate up. His wolf growled, the canines he'd restrained in the cage punched through his gums. "Fuck!"

Leaving the crowded club behind, his blood boiling at the thoughts running through his mind, and not the least calmed from his fight, damn it.

In that moment he could have turned and walked away, forgot everything except getting drunk and patching up his side. Except, he got a glimpse of Breezy's face. Her bruised and swollen face.

He found himself in front of her, forcing Coti back several feet. "Bella, who did this?" He looked at his own bloody hands as he reached up to touch her, hesitating for only a second.

"I don't know," she whispered.

Xan didn't scent a lie, but the smell that he inhaled was of an unknown male. He memorized it, locked it inside himself and knew he and his wolf would hunt the man down.

"You're scary when you look like that."

For her he pushed the feral beast back. "Let me wash up and I'll be right back. You," he stabbed a finger at Coti. "See if there were cameras in the parking garage."

Coti nodded. "On it."

"I thought I was the boss." Kellen drawled.

Xan flipped Kellen off as he entered the large bathroom, shutting the door in order to give himself and his wolf a moment to collect themselves.

Mate. He'd fought the knowledge, thinking he could fuck his way through a dozen or more women and his wolf would forget the one meant to be his. The pain he'd caused her tasted like ash in his mouth. Honesty made him acknowledge he'd known for over a year.

Funny how almost having her taken from him brought clarity, and it didn't seem like a fate worse than death to have her for a mate.

He shucked his clothes and took a quick shower, washing the sweat and blood off. As he got out he looked at the bloody jeans, and decided he'd grab a pair of leathers out of the closet, but first he'd check on Breezy.

With a towel around his hips, he stepped out of the bathroom, glad to see Coti was nowhere to be found. Which meant his friend could breathe another day.

"What the hell, Xan. You forget to put some clothes on or what?" Kellen asked from his spot on the large leather sofa.

Xan smiled. "No, and no you can't see my junk. You'll get all jealous and need someone to feed your ego and tell you yours is big, too." He noticed Breezy had a glass of something cold in her hand.

He grabbed a tumbler and filled it, then held it up to see if Kellen wanted one. A shake of the head and he pushed away from the bar, needing to get close to his woman. Understanding how the mated males were overly possessive of their females, when even the image of another putting their hands on Breezy caused a red hot rage in him.

His words made the people in the room laugh. He, who was not one to make jokes. Beat the shit out of others, and even kill, but joking was not what he was known for.

Her face was already starting to heal thanks to their shifter genetics, but as he stared, she winced when she yawned. As an RN she was on duty for twelve hour shifts and more than likely was ready to fall asleep where she sat.

"I'll take you home, just give me a moment to get dressed." He ran a hand over her soft curls.

"That won't be necessary." Her head swiveled around, following him.

Nudity wasn't a big deal with shifters. He let the towel drop as he opened the closet, selecting a pair of leather pants and pulling them on. He felt her eyes on his ass. No blushing for his woman.

Once he had the pants buttoned, he returned to where she sat sipping her glass of water. "You ready?"

She put the glass down with a clink. "I can't leave my car here. What about when I need to leave?"

Xander was truly beginning to believe he was falling head over ass for her. "When you're ready, I'll take you. Until this bastard is caught, consider me your chauffeur."

Jett's Wild Wolf
Mystic Wolves Book 3
Elle Boon

Prologue

Taryn Cole felt the first skitter of fear slither down her spine as Keith pinned her with his black eyes. The man who claimed her as his daughter, or as one of his possessions, gave her one of his death stares. Others in the great room either dropped to their knees, or showed him their throats, but she did neither, barely resisting the urge.

"Where have you been, little girl?" Keith's voice grated like nails against concrete.

She'd learned at a very young age not to allow him to see how he affected her. A deep inhale helped steady her nerves. "My truck broke down." As long as she stayed close to the truth, Keith wouldn't scent a lie. Another thing she'd learned at his knee, fists, and claws.

Keith cleared the ten or so feet separating them in one leap, startling a gasp out of her. "Don't lie to me you little bitch. I know there was more to it than that. You were in the woods up in Mystic again. Which one of those bastards were you sniffing after?"

His face had contorted into his half-beast. A cross between wolf and whatever he could be. Even Taryn had no clue what all he was, but he was mean.

Her head tilted toward the two wolves standing off to the side. "I followed those two, yes." Again, half truths.

His chest expanded with his deep inhale. She was sure he'd give her some mundane chore, or take away her privileges like a child. At twenty-five years old, being treated like a five year old on a weekly basis was nothing new.

As his large arm raised with its muscles and veins covered by fur, she didn't flinch as he ran the back of his knuckles down her cheek. "Your skin is so smooth, and soft. Unblemished from time and age. Do you know how lucky you are to have my genes coursing through your veins?"

She swallowed. "Yes, alpha." Nobody could accuse her of being a stupid wolf. Her eyes stayed below his chin, yet she never gave him the respect due his status.

"When will you learn your place?" His voice

didn't raise. One claw scraped down, lifting her chin to meet his eyes.

The hate and loathing staring back at her made her gut clench. Whether it was directed at her or the Mystic Wolves didn't matter. Alpha Keith was angry, or suspicious.

Her voice came out a croak. "I don't have a place. I'm the lowest member of your pack, below even that."

The blow that knocked her across the room shocked her, then the pain hit, blood filling her mouth. Before she could get to her feet, he was on her, his hand gripping her by the throat and lifting her up, dangling her feet off the ground.

The scary beast in front of her drew his arm back, the shifted paw of the wolf was larger than a full grown bear, and he flashed his black claws like they were knives. They reminded Taryn of the movie *Nightmare On Elm Street*, when the killer would taunt his victims before he'd slice the razor sharp talons, gutting them. Some days she wondered if he'd actually kill her. Had silently prayed for death on more than one occasion.

He laughed. "Oh, you are truly smart. Too smart maybe."

A rake of those too sharp claws swiped across her cheek, burning her flesh like liquid acid pouring down on her. Silently she screamed, knowing he fed off the pain and anguish of others. Oh, he loved to see his handy work, too. She watched satisfaction flare in his unholy black orbs at the blood running down her face, ruining one of her favorite shirts.

Still, she dangled a good three feet off the ground. His grip on her shirt never loosening while he held her at his height of over six feet four, give or take, in human form, but in his beast mode he was closer to seven.

His next blow broke several ribs, a gasp escaping before she could control it.

"Ah, let's see how much more you can stand. Hmm?" Keith asked, dropping her from his grasp.

Taryn tried to protect her head, knowing it was the most important part of her body. Everything else would heal itself within hours with no outward sign of damage. However, a head injury could take days.

The sound of the pack cheering Keith on became background noise as he continued to kick and hit her. She tried to curl into a ball, focusing all her energy on keeping her head from taking any of his abuse. Every now and again he'd give a grunt, but even that was for show. By the time he was finished, Taryn couldn't count the number of broken bones in her body on both hands.

Excruciating pain radiated out of every pore of her being. Both eyes had swollen to slits from the kicks to her face. Whatever had angered him, Keith had decided she was going to be his punching bag tonight. Not an uncommon occurrence, but this was one of the worst beatings she'd suffered in years. This time she didn't have a mother figure willing to crawl over and help her back to their rooms.

"Someone help the whelp up before I kill her this time. It's not her day to die, yet." He growled, sounding more beast than man.

She wanted to tell whoever came to drag her up to leave her alone, but the gentle touch and sweet scents of her friends washed over her. They hadn't been in the space when Taryn had been summoned by Keith, otherwise her friends would've tried to intervene. They'd have been hurt even worse than her, only their injuries wouldn't have healed as fast, nor as completely.

Joni and Sky eased their arms under her, their wolf strength gave them the ability to lift her with ease. When they reached the sparse room she called her own, they lay her on the full sized bed. A moan finally escaping her busted lips. "Could you get me a glass of water, please?" Was that her voice? She hoped they understood the garbled mess.

Her friend Sky rushed to the small room, not bothering to turn the light on. The cup shook in the other girl's hand. "You look so bad, Ryn."

It hurt to swallow, let alone to reassure her friends she'd be okay. They didn't know how fast she would heal. Heck, she wasn't sure how quickly it would take this time. "Need, time, ladies."

"We are staying with you, so shut the hell up. I brought wine," Joni whispered.

Too tired and hurting to argue, Taryn took another drink of water. Lying on her bed, knowing she was ruining the beautiful bedding, she wanted to cry. A weakness Keith would love to see. Already bones were realigning, bruised organs healing. The last parts of her to heal would be the outer package, which could take days. Days of agony where she would feel each bone and cartilage reform, refill with fresh blood and tissue. Her mind shut down as her last thought was of the alluring wolf Jett Tremaine. Goddess, but he was a fine specimen she'd love to do dirty things to.

The next time she woke it didn't feel like she'd been run over by a Mack Truck, and then backed over again. Lifting her eyelids, she risked a glance down her body, expecting to see blood crusted over every inch of her.

"Thank you jeezus. I didn't think you'd ever wake the fuck up. I swear you scared like ten years off my life," Joni said, coming to stand beside her, a glass in her hand.

It took Taryn a couple seconds to get her voice to work, and then she was able to speak. "How long was I out?"

"Three mother fucking days," Sky growled.

Taryn tried to sit up at the announcement, but the world spun a little. "What? I didn't wake at all?"

"I almost hauled your ass in to the hospital. One more day and you were going." Joni held the drink out, the anxiety she'd obviously felt clear in her tone. "Drink this, and then you need to eat, and no you didn't wake."

Gulping the orange juice down her parched throat, Taryn was glad her friends had stayed with her.

"How do you feel?" Sky asked.

The thought of moving her body didn't appeal in

the least, but Taryn was no pussy. She stretched her legs out, expecting a little pain. When none came she tested her arms, again no pain.

"We took turns watching you, making sure none of the assholes decided to come in and take advantage of you. The second day we decided to wash you up a bit. I couldn't stand to look at the blood on you a moment longer, but we didn't want to jar you too much. Do you think you're up for a bath?" Sky was the mothering sort. Someday she'd make a great mate, just not to one of the jackholes in their pack.

A bath sounded divine, but her rooms didn't boast that extravagance, only a small stand up shower cubicle. Not that she wasn't completely healed, her friends just didn't know that. Both Sky and Joni had better accommodations than she had due to their parents being higher up in Keith's hierarchy. Their alpha would still slit their throats if he felt like it, but he needed them since they provided money to their pack. Sky's parents were lawyers, a needed attribute in their world, while Joni's were the technical geeks who kept Keith up on the latest gadgets. They were like the step sisters in the fairytale, while she was Cinderella. The thought made her giggle. She had no prince charming who would ride in to save her. One day her time would come, when Keith decided she wasn't worth keeping alive and end her. Until then she would enjoy what life she had, and lying around in bloody clothes, stinking to high heaven wasn't on the agenda.

She wished she could hang out with them like regular girls. Go out and have drinks. Dance at the clubs and meet guys. Their world wasn't normal. Sky and Joni's parents would never allow their girls to go anywhere with Keith's thing. Their fear for what he'd do to them if something happened to her, or their hate for her because of what she was made it impossible. Taryn accepted the fact she had no pack outside of her rooms. Joni and Sky loved her as much as they could, would even go against their parents if her life was at stake, which they'd obviously done to stay with her. But she'd never put them in danger. Again. They couldn't handle the beatings she could from Keith. Seeing their pain was worse than feeling her own.

No, Taryn would rather be friendless than have to witness Sky or Joni's tears, or hear the sound of their bones being broken.

If you enjoyed these sneak peeks, be sure to check them out at any ebook retailer. Also catch all the other great reads from Best Selling Author Elle Boon by signing up for her newsletter:

www.elleboon.com/newsletter

About Elle Boon

Elle Boon lives in Middle-Merica as she likes to say...with her husband, her youngest child Goob while her oldest daughter Jazz set out on her own. Oh, and a black lab named Kally Kay who is not only her writing partner but thinks she's human. She'd never planned to be a writer, but when life threw her a curve, she swerved with it, since she's athletically challenged. She's known for saying "Bless Your Heart" and dropping lots of F-bombs, but she loves where this new journey has taken her.

She writes what she loves to read, and that's romance, whether it's about Navy SEALs, or paranormal beings, as long as there is a happily ever after. Her biggest hope is that after readers have read one of her stories, they fall in love with her characters as much as she did. She loves creating new worlds, and has more stories just waiting to be written. Elle believes in happily ever afters, and can guarantee you will always get one with her stories.

Connect with Elle online, she loves to hear from you:

www.elleboon.com

www.facebook.com/elleboon

twitter.com/elleboon

Author's Note

I'm often asked by wonderful readers how they could help get the word out about the book they enjoyed. There are many ways to help out your favorite author, but one of the best is by leaving an honest review. Another great way is spread the word by recommending the books you love, because stories are meant to be shared. Thank you so very much for reading this book and supporting all authors. If you'd like to find out more about Elle's books, visit her website, or follow her on FaceBook, Twitter and other social media sites.

Other Books by Elle Boon

Erotic Ménage
Ravens of War
Selena's Men
Two For Tamara
Jaklyn's Saviors
Kira's Warriors

Shifters Romance
Mystic Wolves
Accidentally Wolf & His Perfect Wolf (1 Volume)
Jett's Wild Wolf
Bronx's Wounded Wolf

Paranormal Romance
SmokeJumpers
FireStarter
Berserker's Rage
A SmokeJumpers Christmas
Mind Bender, Coming Soon

MC Shifters Erotic
Iron Wolves MC
Lyric's Accidental Mate
Xan's Feisty Mate
Kellen's Tempting Mate
Slater's Enchanted Mate
Dark Lovers
Bodhi's Synful Mate
Turo's Fated Mate

Contemporary Romance

Miami Nights
Miami Inferno
Rescuing Miami, Dallas Fire & Rescue

Standalone
Wild and Dirty, Wild Irish Series

SEAL Team Phantom Series
Delta Salvation
Delta Recon
Delta Rogue
Mission Saving Shayna, Omega Team
Protecting Teagan, Special Forces
Delta Redemption

The Dark Legacy Series
Dark Embrace

CPSIA information can be obtained
at www.ICGtesting.com
Printed in the USA
LVHW04s2030130918
590069LV00013B/939/P